Big Doings in Cheyenne...

"You newspaper gents won't want to miss it. We're building a new patent gallows that hangs twentieth century scientifical. They may think they're the bee's knees back in New York State with their new electrical chair. But I guess we keeps up to date in Wyoming."

Interested despite himself, Stringer asked for further details and was assured their wondrous new gallows worked on the principles of a flush toilet. The man sounded as if he could hardly wait to see it work. "The hangman pulls this here chain, as if he was taking a crap, and the rest is all automatical..."

Also in the STRINGER series from Charter

**STRINGER
STRINGER ON DEAD MAN'S RANGE
STRINGER ON THE ASSASSINS' TRAIL**

LOU CAMERON
STRINGER
AND THE HANGMAN'S RODEO

CHARTER BOOKS, NEW YORK

STRINGER AND THE HANGMAN'S RODEO

A Charter Book / published by arrangement with
the author

PRINTING HISTORY
Charter edition / January 1988

All rights reserved.
Copyright © 1988 by Lou Cameron.
This book may not be reproduced in whole
or in part, by mimeograph or any other means,
without permission. For information address:
The Berkley Publishing Group,
200 Madison Avenue, New York, N.Y. 10016.

ISBN: 0-441-79078-X

Charter Books are published by The Berkley Publishing Group,
200 Madison Avenue, New York, N.Y. 10016.
The name "CHARTER" and the "C" logo are trademarks belonging
to Charter Communications, Inc.

PRINTED IN THE UNITED STATES OF AMERICA

10 9 8 7 6 5 4 3 2 1

STRINGER
AND THE HANGMAN'S RODEO

CHAPTER ONE

Stringer was finding it hard to decide what a gent should wear to dinner in Cheyenne these days, since these days included the new Cheyenne Frontier Days and Rodeo he'd been sent to cover by the *San Francisco Sun*.

As he stared down from the window of his hired room on the top floor of the Drover's Palace, the tall sandy-haired newspaperman and erstwhile cowhand decided it made the most sense and the most comfort to go along with the majority. For out front, even though the downtown street was paved and at least half a dozen horseless carriages were parked along the cement curbing, he could see a canvas-covered prairie schooner racing a red river cart down the center of the street. Most of the old boys shouting encouragement from either walk were dressed more wild and woolly than they might have been back when William F. Cody was shooting buffalo more regular on the rolling prairie just outside of town.

As he hauled on the faded denim outfit that still worked best for him in cattle country Stringer reflected on the fact that he and Cheyenne were about the same age. The Union Pacific had laid out the Wyoming township about the time Stringer was born on a hardscrabble spread in the Mother Lode country a mite further west.

Since then they'd both watched thirty-odd years of history go by, and, while some of it had been almost as wild as old Ned Buntline liked to tell it in his wild west magazines, Stringer was more inclined to look forward into the dawning twentieth century than he was to dwell on the past. Had it been up to him, he'd be further east right now, covering features like the new moving pictures they were starting to make in Jersey State, or those Ohio brothers who were said to be working on a flying machine. But it wasn't up to him. His feature editor, Sam Barca, kept sending him to cover rodeos and such because he felt a writer who'd grown up sort of cow and ducked a few rounds in the Spanish American War might notice wild west details a more city-bred reporter might miss. Stringer didn't know what he was supposed to look for. These newfangled rodeo rules, as far as he understood them, didn't make much sense. Back when he'd been learning to stay aboard a bronc, the only rule had been to keep the infernal brute from throwing you. Nobody had said word one about making it any tougher than it already was. And nobody working on a real spread would have been *allowed* to try that with a beef critter, as they did now. The whole point had been to raise beef as fat as possible, not to worry the fool cows skinny.

Stringer grumped into his spurred Justins and put on the beat-up Roughrider hat he'd brought home from Cuba as he considered the gun rig spread across the bed covers for a time. Half the old boys whooping things up downstairs seemed to be packing guns this afternoon, whatever the Cheyenne ordinances might read on less boisterous occasions. But it seemed a mite dramatic to wear a sidearm to dinner smack in the middle of a good-sized and fairly civilized community.

On the other hand, there was no call to act like a spoilsport and, what the hell, Butch and Sundance had last been seen less than a thousand miles from Cheyenne. So Stringer grinned sheepishly and wrapped the rig around his lean denim-clad hips, adjusting his S&W double-action .38 to ride more comfortably against his right thigh. Then he adjusted the black silk bandana he was wearing in place of a necktie and locked up to go downstairs.

The hotel dining room was just off the lobby. But before he could get there a desk clerk called him over to say there was a message for him. As Stringer waited for the clerk to hand him a slip of paper, a shingle, or whatever, the clerk explained, "One of the guards at the Cheyenne Jail left word for you—informal—Mister MacKail. He said, if you had the time, old Tom Horn had asked if you'd be good enough to drop by and hear his sad story."

Stringer frowned thoughtfully, dredged up the name from the many a good newspaper man had to remember, and muttered, "I fear I've heard it, if we're talking about that sordid killing a spell back. Isn't Tom Horn the morose individual who gunned down a young sheepherder somewhere around here?"

The room clerk nodded and didn't seem much more interested as he replied, "Yep. Willie Nickell was the boy's name, and you're right about it being sordid. We don't book rooms to sheepherders here. But just the same, Tom Horn had no call to throw down on a fourteen-year-old boy, even if he'd been armed, which Willie Nickell was not. That's why they got Tom Horn over to the jail, waiting to swing for it. It wouldn't do to hang a man during the current festivities, with tourists in town and all."

Stringer thanked the clerk for the information and went on

in to enjoy his dinner. But while the steak and potatoes were all right, and the coffee was really good, Stringer didn't enjoy himself enough to order dessert. One part of him kept saying there was no point depressing himself further about the banalities of a solved and settled case that hadn't looked too interesting when he'd first read of it in a rival paper many moons ago. But another part of him kept saying a man about to die was surely good for a more interesting interview than a man about to get bucked off a horse. So after rolling a smoke at the table and then picking up most of his change, Stringer headed for the jail house, near the railroad depot.

He was starting to feel sorry, however, even before they let him in to see the doomed gunslick. The sun was going down, and as if to make the gloom more depressing, they not only made him take off his gun rig out front but patted him down for other weapons. When he protested, one of the guards explained, not unkindly, that it wouldn't be the first time old Tom had tried to slicker the law, and that it was a simple fact he rode with a good-sized gang.

As another guard led Stringer down along a dark, dank corridor he was asked if he meant to cover the hanging of their prisoner as well. When Stringer replied, "Not if I can help it," the lawman answered in an injured tone, "You newspaper gents won't want to miss it. We're building a new patent gallows that hangs twentieth century scientifical. They may think they're the bee's knees back in New York State with their new electrical chair. But I guess we keeps up to date in Wyoming."

Interested despite himself, Stringer asked for further details and was assured their wondrous new gallows worked on the principles of a flush toilet. The guard sounded as if he could hardly wait to see it work. "The hangman pulls this here chain, as if he was taking a crap, and the rest is all automatical, run by hydraulic whatever. Soon as the water runs from one tank into another, the trap is sprung and..."

"Jesus," Stringer cut in, "you mean the condemned man gets to stand there, listening to them sort of flush his life away?"

"Yep," the guard said. "Takes about a minute and a half. But of course the rascal don't know just when the trap under him is fixing to spring. It's supposed to be sort of a surprise, see?"

"I see how it could give a man about to hang more than enough time to contemplate the error of his ways. And you say it's supposed to be more civilized than the old-fashioned way?"

The guard insisted Wyoming had to move with the times and they stopped by a solid door of oak sheathed with sheet iron. He unlocked it, saying, "There you go. I'll be back in, say, ten minutes to see if old Tom has kilt you." And then Stringer was inside and the door was closed, and bolted behind him.

But as his eyes adjusted to the dismal light Stringer saw he'd been locked in with a skinny middle-aged gent who looked more forlorn than ferocious.

The soon-to-be late Tom Horn had never been taught to cry, and since he had nothing to smile about he just sat woodenly on his cot, nervously braiding a handsome black and white rope of horsehair. His own hairline was receding and his John L. Sullivan moustache drooped as if he'd just been licked. Neither man said anything for a time. Then Horn moved his rump and his coils of rope to make room on the only seat in the cell, saying, "I've read your stuff in the papers, if I'm correct in taking you for the Mister Stuart MacKail who signs his work as Stringer."

Stringer got out the makings for a smoke, then sat down

beside the older man. "That byline is a sort of inside newspaper joke," he said. "Care for some tobacco, Mister Horn?"

The prisoner shook his head and answered, "You go on 'n roll. I gave up smoking a spell back. What I'd really like right now is some raw bacon. You ever chaw raw bacon, Mister MacKail?"

"I don't even chaw tobacco. I never can find a place to spit."

"I know. That's how come I chaws bacon to steady my nerves. You get to swallow all you have to and it don't make you sick."

Stringer had serious reservations about that. But he just put together a smoke as he asked, "What was it you wanted to see me about, Mister Horn? I'm sure you're innocent, but, no offense, you had your say in court and they did find you guilty."

Horn just shrugged. "I never gunned that kid. Honest. But that ain't why I wanted to tell my tale to a newspaper man. You see, all during the trial, I kept waiting for my pals to come forward and alibi me. But they never did and I've been sitting here ever since, wondering why. I hate to say it about old pards, Mister MacKail, but the closer I get to them gallows the more it looks to me that I been throwed to the wolves."

Stringer licked his cigarette paper to seal it before he asked just who they were talking about.

"I ain't ready to say," Horn answered, "not just yet. I always thought they was my friends. Mayhaps they still is. But would you let a friend hang if a word from you could get him off, Mister MacKail?"

Stringer struck a match and lit the twisted end of his smoke. "Well, not hardly," he said. "Are you suggesting these mysterious friends of yours could be letting you take the fall for killing Willie Nickell because they're covering for the real killer?"

Tom Horn shook his head. "I fail to see how they'd know more about it than I do," he said. "None of us was anywhere near the Iron Mountain range when that boy was murdered. We was all...ah...tending other chores for the C.P.A. at the time."

Stringer tried to hurry the laconic older man up by running a few yards with the ball himself. "Let's see if I remember the case we're jawing about. The C.P.A. would be the Cattleman's Protective Association, and you and these mysterious pals of yours would be hired guns for the same, right?"

Tom Horn grimaced and said, "I'd rather you called me a range detective, Mister MacKail. Hired gun sounds a mite harsh."

"Harsh is as harsh does," Stringer shrugged. "We're not going to get anyplace if we bullshit one another, Mister Horn. I may as well tell you right out that I have it on good authority that you, Tom Horn, have been known to leave an occasional enemy of your employers dead as a cow turd on the lone prairie. By the way, where did you ever come up with that notion of leaving a rock under their heads as a sort of pillow—or is that meant to be your calling card?"

Tom Horn sighed sheepishly. "I only done that a time or two as a sort of joke. I can't rightly say why it seemed all that humorous at the time."

Stringer grimaced. "Correct me if I'm wrong," he said flatly, "but isn't it a fact that they found young Willie Nickell in not-so-sweet repose with a big flat rock under his head? And isn't it just as true that you'd had words with his father on the subject of sheep, not long before the kid was shot down like a dog in the cold gray dawn?"

"I can see you read up on the subject," Horn replied. "That was just the way them other reporters writ it. But I thought you was a *fair* reporter, Mister MacKail. I only sent for you, as soon as I heard you was in town, because I read some of the stories about the War when we was all down Cuba-way, and you was about the only one there who told things the way they was happening."

Stringer felt a shade of satisfaction at the too-obvious compliment, then shrugged it off fast. "President Roosevelt has assured me he's forgiven me for writing the truth about San Juan Hill," he said. "But let's get back to more recent foolishness. Are you trying to tell me lies were printed about you and that young sheepherder?"

Horn nodded. "Not outright mean lies. But you know how dumb greenhorns write about the way things really is in cow country, Mister MacKail. To begin with, I've never denied I knew that's boy's father, old Kell Nickell. But not to have words with him. Coffee and cake was more like it, on the occasions I stopped by. I ain't asking you to buy that because you like me. I want you to stop and ask yourself why a range detective for the C.P.A. would have anything to fuss about with him and his fool kid."

"Weren't they running sheep?"

"Well, sure they was, on their own land. The Nickells wasn't herding sheep serious on any open range the C.P.A. would give a damn about. Old Kell Nickell stayed put on his quarter-section homestead claim. His sheep was *fenced in*. Didn't it say right out in them papers you read that the dead boy was found by their open gate?"

Stringer raised an eyebrow, blew a thoughtful smoke ring, and decided for himself. "All right. Let's say the victim was a homesteader who kept sheep, instead of a sheepherder on range someone else might have thought the Lord meant for cows. How do you explain that stone pillow under his head—if you didn't put her there?"

Tom Horn wiped his face with a big raw-boned hand and sniffed. "I can't explain it. I can't even say it was there. It wasn't mentioned in the papers when they first found the boy dead. It was later, after I'd been arrested for a killing I had no hand in, that some sassy reporters commenced to say such a memento was my trademark. You just read the minutes of my trial if you think I left Willie Nickell dead with a fool rock under his head. And if you can find me that rock, presented as evidence in court, I'll be proud to eat it for you—without no cream or sugar!"

Stringer took another long drag on his smoke before speaking his mind. "It's a mite late to go over evidence that might or might not have been used against you in court," he finally said. "What the prosecution presented, the judge and jury bought. I'm no lawyer, Horn, but if you aim to get off on appeal, you'd better get cracking with some new evidence to argue about."

"What if I could prove I was riding with some other gents, in other parts, doing other things at the time?" Horn asked. "That ought to do her," Stringer replied, flicking an ash, "assuming it doesn't get you all locked up for another crime. Are you saying that's why these mysterious pals of yours refuse to come forward for you?"

Horn nodded weakly. "I reckon it has to be. We never done nothing more serious than a little cutting and burning. Would you let a pard hang for a crime he never done, if all they could give you was, say, a year at hard?"

Stringer whistled softly and said, "Oh, boy. If you're telling half the truth, I feel for you. But I'd sure have to like you a lot more than I do right now before I'd spend a year or more in prison for you."

Tom Horn scowled down at the cement floor and growled, "Some gents just don't seem to savvy friendship, then. For we ain't just talking a spell in jail with time-off for decent manners. The State of Wyoming means to hang me high, for a killing I had no hand in. You got to get my old pards to come forward, see?"

"Not hardly," Stringer replied, "if you won't even tell me who the hell they are."

"I can't peach on pards," Horn said. "That's against the code. But what if you was to print something in your paper for 'em to read?"

"I'm afraid I don't handle classified ads for the *Sun*."

"I mean a warning to 'em, from me, right on the front page, see? I want you to put it in the papers that if they mean to let me down I just might have some mean things to say about them all, naming names, when that hangman asks if I got any last words."

Stringer thought about that as he finished a last few puffs of Bull Durham. Then he dropped the butt on the floor, ground it out with his boot, and got to his feet. "I can't promise anything. But I will ask my editor if we can run your message, Mister Horn."

The older man got to his feet as he said, "Call me Tom, seeing we was in Cuba together." But Stringer just felt sort of shitty as the two of them shook on it to part friendly. For Stringer knew that even if he made such a suggestion to old Sam Barca by wire, his crusty boss would answer with a roar that would hardly require the services of Western Union. The *San Francisco Sun* printed news. There was no news in a convicted murderer saying he was innocent. Now there might have really been something had old Tom Horn wanted to make a full confession, clearing up those loose ends that always seemed to be left over.

Out front, as they gave Stringer his gun rig back, one of the guards asked, "What did he want to tell you? That same old bull about his old night-riding pards ganging up with the law to do him dirty?"

Stringer strapped his gun back on, then he nodded. "That was about the size of it. We never got into why you boys arrested him in the first place."

Another guard snorted in disgust, then protested, "Hell, it was U.S. Marshal Joe LeFors that arrested Horn, and, if you want to know why, it was because LeFors heard it from the horse's mouth."

"You mean someone *saw* Tom Horn kill Willie Nickell?"

"Sure I do. Tom Horn himself. Joe LeFors never would have arrested him if he hadn't outright confessed to the killing while they was drinking together. I reckon old Tom lost track of who he was drinking with at the time. It was only when he sobered some that old Tom commenced to come up with mysterious pards who could alibi him, if only they would. You ain't the first reporter he's pulled the same yarn on. How come you're looking at *us* so mean? It wasn't *our* notion to green you so, old son."

CHAPTER TWO

The summer night was brightly lit, even if it was still young. Someone in Cheyenne had gotten a real buy on Edison bulbs. Stringer put the pathetic protests of poor old Tom Horn aside as he followed the jam-packed Main Street toward the fair grounds. He smiled thinly as he regarded the whopping wonder of modern electrical science they'd strung high across the street ahead. For while all those winking dots of white light were no doubt meant to spell out "POWDER RIVER AND LET HER BUCK!" some prankster with a tolerable aim had shot out some of the bulbs forming the *B*, to turn it into an *F*. But none of the gals promenading at this hour let on they noticed.

Stringer noticed most of the gals were dressed like the modern Gibson Girl, even if the fair was supposed to be the Cheyenne of at least a generation ago. Some of the men made up for it by wearing outfits the late James Butler Hickock would have found a mite old-fashioned the day he died in '76. Stringer figured about half the men he passed had some notion which end of a horse was which. It took practice to walk natural in high heels and spurs. It was safe to assume that even when a man managed to walk cow, he still had to be a banker or at least a well-paid clerk when he came swaggering down the walk in beaded white buckskins or white angora chaps. For no working hand could afford the regular dry cleaning, and the smell of mothballs coming from a passing forty-niner was an even more obvious give-away.

But as Stringer got closer to the fair grounds the crowd began to thin and give way to the real thing. For they were only putting on the shows by daylight. So anyone working or hanging about after dark tended to take the cattle industry a mite more serious.

You didn't need a ticket to pass through the unguarded gate after dark. The bleachers and most of the tanbark patch the size of a football field were barely visible by moonlight, of course, but down at the chute-end Stringer saw that, sure enough, a modest crowd was assembled under a string of overhead bulbs. Most of them seemed to be just perched on rails, but something was going on in one of the chutes. So Stringer sauntered closer to see what was up.

As he drew closer to the light a voice he sincerely hoped was not as familiar as it sounded called out, "Hey, ain't you good old Stu MacKail from Calaveras County?" Without waiting for an answer, it added, "There goes your prize money, boys. For with two California riders in the contest the rest of you is doomed."

Stringer was close enough now to see there was just no way of avoiding the fact it was old Swede Larson, off the Tumbled T Bar X just down the other side of Angels Camp. The big blond moose was one of those jovial bully boys a man just never knew whether he was supposed to laugh at or to punch. In his time, Stringer had done both on a Saturday night with Swede Larson. So far, they were about even. Swede had cold-cocked Stringer that one time and the next time Stringer had kicked the shit out of him. He could only hope the muscular moron wasn't looking for a rematch. Old Swede fought southpaw and seemed to be a sucker for a right cross. But chopping down anything that big was still a tedious chore.

As Stringer joined the group he ignored the hand Swede Larson held out to him. Letting a left-handed cold-cocker grab your own right fist could be a big mistake. But if Larson was insulted he failed to show it. He settled for corking Stringer's shoulder, hard, and bellowing, "I want you all to howdy my old pard, Stu MacKail, from back home. Now that he's here, you boys who've entered the saddle bronc events might as well go on home. For I have seen this boy ride and, like the song says, there was never a pony that couldn't be rode and there was never a rider that couldn't be throwed. But they wasn't aware of this rider when they writ a dumb thing like that."

A couple of the other hands nodded pleasantly enough. Some others just looked through him, and a pretty gal perched atop a rail in split leather skirts and a white Texas hat just sniffed down at him as if he needed a bath.

The object of her scorn laughed lightly and said, "You've got things wrong more ways than one, Swede. In the first place, it's just not my fault my folk named me after the losing side in the history of their old country. Stuart is bad enough. Stu sounds like hobo grub. So my real pals call me Stringer."

"How come, Stu?" Larson asked.

"'Cause that's what I do for a living and that takes us to the second place. I'm not here to ride against you boys. I'm covering the big show as a stringer or field reporter for the *San Francisco Sun*," Stringer said.

One of the strangers in the crowd snorted, "Shoot, we might have knowed a dumb Swede couldn't tell a pencil pusher from a cowhand."

"Oh, yeah, now I recall," Larson growled. "They told me, back home, that you'd run off to college to learn about big words. I reckon honest cow punching just wasn't good enough for you high and mighty MacKails, huh?"

"Leave my clan out of it," Stringer said flatly, "unless you've improved your guard a mite. I didn't come here to rawhide or be rawhided, Swede. So let's talk about more interesting events. What are those boys doing back there in the chutes? I can't make it out in this light."

Larson didn't answer. He was probably trying to make up his mind about Stringer's vicious right cross. A somewhat kinder sounding hand explained, "Old Stardust busted through a partition and the wranglers are trying to put him back to bed without busting him up or vice versa."

Another with a Texas drawl volunteered, "My money is on the bronc." So Stringer moved closer, put a boot up on a rail, and hoisted his head and shoulders up in line with the leather-clad rump of the snippy young gal facing the other way. She paid no mind to him, so he studied what seemed to be going on in the inky shadows on the far side. Four or maybe five husky hands were wrestling with a black brute big enough to haul a beer wagon, and Stringer could see the man from Texas had a point. Old Stardust wasn't fighting them as much as he was pretending to be an immovable object. But as one of them made the mistake of moving between the big stud's shoulder and the rails, Stardust suddenly shifted his considerable weight to bust the man's backbone like a twig—and might have if the wrangler hadn't been smart enough to roll through, instead of against, the rails. "Hold him, boys!" the wrangler shouted. "He's loose on my side and premeditating murder again!"

"Yeah, that one's a man killer all right," Stringer remarked to the girl, but she didn't answer. So he climbed back down and tried to see if anyone else would answer his observations. "I'd sure hate to see a friend of mine draw a ride like that critter seems to be offering. Have they told you who gets to ride old Stardust, Swede?"

Larson shook his head and replied, "They ain't got to the saddle bronc drawings yet. The event don't start until day-after-tomorrow. They put on lots of silly stuff first. They have to hold this big parade with covered wagons, wild Indians, and a mess of flags. Then Miss Rimfire Rowena, here, gets to ride all over creation shooting at balls."

There was a muffled round of laughter before the girl perched atop the rail sniffed and protested, "I shoot Christmas tree balls from the saddle, hanging or throwed."

"She's Montana's answer to Annie Oakley," said the Texas hat. But a taller, leaner and less friendly sounding rider opined, "She's younger and prettier than Annie Oakley, but she misses a lot more often if you ask me."

Rimfire Rowena snapped, "Nobody's asking you, Lash Borden, and even if they were, you'd still be full of it. I guess *I* know who Miss Annie Oakley refused to compete against that time at the Omaha State Fair and, besides, she cheats. Anyone can bust glass balls and balloons with birdshot rounds from a big old dragoon conversion. I aim bullets, fair and square. So it stands to pure reason a gal has to miss now and again."

Stringer felt sorry for the pretty little thing, even if she was sort of snippy, so he said, "Let's get back to the saddle bronc riding. That would be what you're here for, right, Swede? Lord knows you never could rope worth a hang."

Larson smiled back, just as friendly, and said, "I guess I could show you a thing or two about roping, if you hadn't run off to a girlish job and let your hands go soft. But seeing as you want to know, I am here for the bucking and I'm here to win."

The Texas hat laughed and said, "Not if you draw Stardust you ain't, Swede. The boy who gets to ride that moonfishing sidewinder can kiss his entry fee *adios*. His doctor bills might well take the rest of his money as well."

Stringer knew a little about the way such riding was judged. "Oh, I don't know. Since the judges give extra points on the way the critter bucks, it seems to me that the rider who draws that big bad bucker ought to wind up with the highest score, if only he can stay aboard until the horn blows."

The Texas hat laughed and said, "You're more than welcome to old Stardust, then. I, for one, like to get off alive, and Stardust don't stop bucking just because he hears the timing horn and feels his bucking cinch fall free. He crippled a rider in Globe last summer, long after they blowed the horn and the side rider uncinched him."

Another hand opined he was sort of hoping for a more civilized mount as well. Then the one called Lash grinned wolfishly at Stringer and said, "I don't see how you boys can offer Stardust to this pencil pusher, boys. He talks a good ride. But I've met many a professor playing piano in a house of ill repute who can *talk* about our trade, with his sissy rump safe on a piano stool."

It got mighty quiet all of a sudden, save for the tugging and cussing on the far side of the rails. Stringer smiled back at Lash politely enough, then gave him his mind. "Every man is entitled to an honest opinion. Since I won't be riding in your rodeo, pard, I won't get the chance to prove you right or wrong."

"Oh, I don't know," Lash countered. "It seems to me it might quiet old Stardust's nerves a mite if he was to get some of his wild oats out of his system afore the official contest."

Then, before anyone could figure out what he meant, Lash moved over to the rails, boosted himself up, and called down to the sweating wranglers on the far side, "Hey, boys, we got us a real rider out here who's just dying to give that brute some fun. What say we let him and old Stardust show us their stuff?"

The head wrangler, wrestling with the big stud's head, called back, "May as well. I'll be damned if I can figure how to get him back in his stall, and this is a bucking shoot."

Rimfire Rowena protested, "Stop it, all of you! Are you trying to get this poor dude killed?"

"Yeah, that's the idea," Larson said, winking. "Somebody get a saddle and we're all set. The critter's already wearing a hackamore."

There was a jovial roar of agreement and at least another half-dozen hands climbed over the rails to help get the man-killer set to fly. The one with the Texas hat sidled up to Stringer and told him gently, "It ain't too late for you to start walking, old son. I don't know what makes Lash so mean, and this just ain't funny."

The girl seemed to be on his side, too, as she dropped down from the rails and confided, "I fear it's partly my fault. You know how silly some boys act in front of girls."

Stringer smiled down at her. It was easy, now that he had a better look at her face. Despite her rough garb and tough talk it was a pretty little cameo-face, framed by soft black hair as well as her ten-gallon hat. "Well," Stringer said, smiling, "I'd walk a picket fence for you if there was one about. But since I don't see any picket fence I'll just have to show off with that stud, won't I?"

She protested, "You don't have to prove anything to me, you big goof. If I say I'm sorry I called you a dude, will you do me a favor and run like hell?"

He laughed, moved around her, and climbed up the rails to call out, "How are you boys coming down there? I haven't got all night."

They'd been coming better than he hoped. Twelve men good and true were simply too many for even a brute like

Stardust to fight off. So the next thing Stringer knew he was lowering himself into the saddle as the bronc tried to bust his kneecaps against the rails on either side. Swede Larson handed him the hackamore line and growled, "Rodeo rules, unless you aim to let Calaveras County down. It's a point against you if you let your rein hand touch the horn, and if you grab it you're disqualified total."

Stringer growled back, "I know the damn rules. Open the damn chute before he busts my damn legs."

But another helpful bastard insisted, "No hanging on with your spurs. Keep your stirrups clear and fanning at all times. You can whup with your hat if you like but if your free hand touches any part of his hide or saddle it's a point against you."

Stringer started to repeat that he damn well knew the way the game was supposed to be played. Just then Lash, who'd been watching for the worst time to do it, sprung the gate and let Stardust spring out of the chute like a hungry lion looking for some poor Christian to eat.

There wasn't one human target left out on the poorly lit tanbark. Everyone had naturally climbed higher than those man-killing hooves could reach. So Stardust proceeded to try to kill the man on his back and, to do that, he naturally had to first buck Stringer off.

Stringer didn't want to be bucked off. So their honest difference of opinion added up to one hell of a show. Stardust was content to aim himself at the overhead moon, shaking like a water spaniel and trying to turn himself inside out, until he saw that wouldn't work. He crow-hopped toward the bleachers and would have amputated Stringer's left leg with the rail in front of the empty seating if Stringer hadn't aimed a boot tip at the moon just in time. Then Stardust bucked another way, swapping ends at the top of each astounding leap, and now most of the bunch were yelling encouragement to Stringer as they saw he was the real thing and then some.

The Texas hat called out, "Time! You've been on him long enough, cowboy! Get off whilst you're still ahead!"

Stringer called back, "How?" as he rode the murderous bronc in a circle of attempted hand stands. He let go his hat and bent low to grope for the bucking cinch that should have been behind his thigh. There wasn't any. Stardust was just murderous by nature, it appeared.

As if to prove it, the big stud did something that was simply against the natural instincts of its species. He threw himself down on the tanbark like a spoiled brat throwing a temper tantrum on the rug and tried to roll over Stringer as if this had become an infernal wrestling match.

Stringer might have wound up dead or worse if he hadn't moved like spit on a hot stove to vacate the saddle and leap over the brute's big belly, between the flailing hooves, to wind up on the off side, still holding the hackamore line. As the man-killer finished his roll and wound up like a big reclining hound dog at Stringer's feet, Stringer punched him in the muzzle and followed up with a hold on the chin strap to keep the brute down. By that time the Texas hat and a couple of other decent cusses, including Rimfire Rowena, had dashed over to pile on and help. As Stringer cupped a palm over Stardust's nostrils to calm him, if he meant to go on breathing at all, the girl unsaddled the big bronc, half sobbing, "Don't you ever do that again!"

Pushing his way in, one of the wranglers yelled up, "Let me get aholt that hack and it may be safe to let him up. He do hate saddles. But bareback again after all that bucking he may just be willing to behave a mite better, now. You sure are a riding fool, Mister MacKail."

The Texas hat laughed and chimed in, "You would have finished in the money if you'd made that ride afore the judges just now. Are you sure you don't want to enter the contest? It ain't too late, you know, and a man who can stay aboard Stardust can surely ride anything else they have to offer here."

Stringer picked up the saddle and didn't argue when the girl gathered up the saddle blanket. He saw the others had the bronc under control. So they all headed sedately back to the chutes. "I'm a newspaper man, not a rodeo rider," Stringer explained, "that is, when I have anything to say about it. Besides, the entry fees are a mite rich for my blood. I might be willing to give it a fling if they let you boys get killed for free. Paying for the privilege has always struck me as sort of dumb, no offense."

By the time they rejoined everyone else at the chute end, the bronc he'd just ridden was acting tame enough to be led in with no further argument. Swede Larson seemed sincere as he slapped Stringer on the back and chortled, "I knew you wouldn't let our home range down." The one called Lash just shrugged and said, "You'd have lost points in a real contest. Any fool can stay on when he keeps his stirrups braced like that."

Stringer didn't answer. He draped the saddle over a rail and turned to take the saddle blanket from the girl. As it slid from her grasp Rimfire Rowena said, "Ouch," and then added, "Say, how come this big old burr was sticking to that saddle blanket? It's no wonder Stardust went pure loco out there just now! I guess I'd buck, too, if I had something like this in my underthings!"

Stringer stared hard at both Swede Larson and Lash Borden, trying to decide which one looked the most homicidal as well as stupid. Lash grinned like a mean little kid and asked, "Can't you take a little joke, pard?" So Stringer unbuckled his gun rig, handed it to Rimfire Rowena, and said, "No," before he swung.

It would have been a mistake to lead with his right. But Lash wasn't any better at ducking a left hook than Swede

Larson was a right cross. So he went down with a split lip, rolled, and as Stringer stepped politely back to let him get back up, Lash did so, with a six-inch boot knife in his right fist.

So the fight might have gotten sort of serious if at this point Rimfire Rowena hadn't pulled Stringer's .38 from its holster and fired it straight into the tanbark between them. "That's enough," she announced, sounding as if she meant it. "If there's one thing I can't abide, it's grown men behaving like schoolboys."

Stringer smiled sheepishly at Lash and said, "I'm willing to call us even if you are." So Lash said, "Jesus, can't nobody take a joke around here?" and put his blade away.

But Stringer knew it might not be over. So he turned back to the girl and told her, "I'd be proud to buy you an ice cream soda if you're headed back to town, ma'am. That's where I'm going, as soon as I can have my gun rig back."

She dimpled up at him despite herself and said, "Only if you promise to be a good boy. What are you doing with real bullets in your sidearm? Didn't anyone tell you Frontier Days was supposed to be just play acting? You like to scared me half to death when I felt the kick of a solid round just now. I was expecting blanks."

As he took the rig from her and strapped it on, Stringer said, "I was raised to treat guns with respect, ma'am. It's just dumb to pack a gun without real bullets in it."

He saw Lash was pouting off at a slow walk now and added, "Do you reckon that's what made him think he could rawhide me in front of you, the notion that I was just a drugstore cowboy with a toy gun?"

She shrugged and answered, "That's what *I* took you for. Half the gents packing guns in town right now have never fired one. As for that ice cream soda, maybe another time. I'm camped down the other way and you may as well know I'm not easy."

Stringer gulped and said, "I don't recall hearing anyone say you were, ma'am."

She sniffed. "I know how men talk about me behind my back, and even in front of me, if I let on I got the double meanings."

"Is that why you talk so tough, Miss Rowena?" he asked.

She shrugged, righting her ten-gallon straight on her forehead. Her soft black curls peeked out from under the rim. "I guess a girl has to learn to talk tough if she means to get ahead in this man's world. The Sioux took my mother's hair when I was maybe one year old. So I was raised by my poor old pappy as best he knew how, until he got run over by a stampede when I was maybe twelve."

"That sure sounds mournsome, ma'am. Who looked after you when you ran out of kin entire?"

"Nobody. I looked after myself and one of the things I taught myself at my own knee was not to take no wooden nickles and not to be easy. I taught myself to shoot as well, and it's a good thing I did. I bet you got no idea how hard it can be for a gal to be good—even when she owns her own guns."

Things were still lively as Stringer got back to the more lit-up parts of Cheyenne. Most of the desperados he passed looked harmless as ever. But he found himself looking harder at them now. Since he'd just learned the first lesson about playacting at wild west notions. Lash Borden had taken him for a playactor wearing his sidearm just for show, and, to be fair, it was an easy enough mistake to make with so many harmless gents playing foolish wild west games these days. But as they had all just learned, the old ways hadn't faded out entirely. They'd just gotten a lot more complicated.

As he passed a brightly illuminated moving picture gallery he could see by the posters that they were running a Pathé travelogue and that new dramatic offering, *The Great Train Robbery*. Stringer had already seen it and it wasn't bad, even though you could tell they'd made it back East in some woods. It was meant as entertainment and the actors hadn't known all that much about robbing real trains, in Stringer's opinion. But this very summer the real Wild Bunch was robbing trains left and right on an almost monotonous basis. It was even possible, with so many folk in town this evening, that right this minute Butch and Sundance were sitting inside, watching *The Great Train Robbery* and no doubt enjoying a chuckle or more.

The times just felt out of joint since Stringer had come home from the Spanish American War. In fact, by now they were taking moving pictures of that new war down there in the Philippines, and if the Paiute didn't watch out they'd wind up on film as well. Having sat out the earlier Indian wars, the Paiute had suddenly taken to raising hell over in the great basin, and the army was talking about using those newfangled machine guns on them if they didn't stop.

As for old-time gunfighters, despite all the fancy new ways of this dawning century, a mess of them were still around. He'd just talked to one in the Cheyenne Jail. So as he saw a moody-looking gent approaching with a tie-down holster Stringer tensed a mite and hankered for the good old days, when a man could tell whether he was supposed to tense or not.

But as he passed the drugstore where he'd meant to buy Rimfire Rowena an ice cream soda, and saw a pair of perky Gibson Girls sipping the same at the marble counter, he decided he might not be in the Dodge of the '80s after all and moved on in restored spirits.

When he got back to his hotel it was still too early to

turn in. So he strolled into the tap room off the other side of the lobby to see what else might be going on.

Nothing was going on at first. There was an upright piano in one corner. But nobody was playing it. He bellied up to the bar and ordered a schooner of beer. Nobody argued about it until he was about half through. Then a voice growled in his ear, "It has ever been my opinion that men who drink nothing stronger than beer sit down to pee."

Stringer put down his schooner and turned wearily to the even taller stranger who'd apparently followed him in, since he hadn't been there before. The somewhat older as well as taller man was wearing a black frock coat under a pancaked black Stetson. The coat was hanging open as if to offer Stringer a clear view of the two ivory-handled Colt Lightnings the gent was wearing as well. Stringer sighed and said, "Look, friend, I just had a fight this evening, and for the record, I won. So why don't you go off and sniff at fire hydrants or something?"

The stranger smiled, almost pleasantly, and replied, "I can see you don't know who you are talking to, Stringer. Does the handle Friendly Frank Folsom mean anything to you?"

The younger newspaperman shook his head and replied, "I can't say it does. Since you seem to know who *I* am, why don't you tell me what this is all about, Friendly Frank?"

The stranger said, "It's your nose, *amigo*. How come it's so big?"

Stringer wrinkled the object under discussion and said, "I thought you were sore at me for drinking beer. How did my poor nose get into this? I'll allow it ain't much. But it's always struck me as a sort of average nose."

"You're wrong," Friendly Frank said. "You keep sticking it in places it don't belong, and I ain't talking about fire hydrants. What makes you so nosy, Stringer?"

"I reckon it goes with my job. Where have I got it stuck right now to upset you so?"

"It ain't me you've been upsetting, Stringer. I'll tell you true I was ordered to pick a fight with you and sort of kill you in self-defense. But, as you may have guessed, I'm a professional, not a homicidal lunatic. So I like to kill folk more discreetly than in the middle of a damned old festival."

Stringer said he was glad to hear that and added, "Maybe some other time and place, after the rodeo is over?"

Friendly Frank said, "They don't want you in Cheyenne that long, Stringer. They told me they wanted you dead or run out of town—tonight. So what's it going to be?"

Then he blanched and went sort of stiff-all-over as he found himself standing there with the muzzle of Stringer's .38 lightly resting against the front of his vest. Stringer asked quietly, "Why don't you tell me what it's going to be?"

Friendly Frank gulped and said, "Jesus H. Christ, they told me you were fast, but that was just impossible. Where on earth did a prissy reporter learn to draw so sudden?"

Stringer put his .38 back in its holster. "Want to see it again? I wasn't always a newspaper man. Since I have been, I've discovered lots of folk don't cotton to my brand of investigative reportage. I can't do much about the son of a bitch who goes over my stuff with a blue pencil. But as I hope you may have surmised by now, I meet lots of assholes like you."

"I can't say I enjoy being called an asshole, Stringer."

"That's too bad. You sure act like one. If you don't like it, slap leather. I don't have to be polite to gents I don't like, and unlike you, I feel perfectly free to blow you away in self-defense because I don't have a record as a hired gun to live down. If you don't want to fight, suppose you tell me now who sent you after me. Call it nosy or not, I want to know, just in case they send a *real* fighter after me next time."

Friendly Frank shook his head and said, "You know I can't tell you that. But if it's any comfort to you, I've just decided to deal myself out. They didn't offer me half the money they should have to take a gunslick like you, even if I still thought I could. So how about it, pard. Is the war over?"

Stringer shook his head and said, "Not yet. I'll be proud to buy you a drink after you tell me who sent you. But if you still try to crawfish out with me in the dark, I'll kill you."

Friendly Frank's face turned an even paler shade of frog belly. But he shook his head and said, "I reckon I'll have to cover that bet. I don't like the odds all that much. But the only other way to go means death for certain. They know where to find me and, worse yet, they know where to find my kin."

Then he simply turned his back on Stringer and started for the nearest exit with his hands up.

Stringer's own hand went for his gun as he snapped, "Hey, come back here, damnit!"

But he didn't draw. Just like Friendly Frank was betting on, Stringer was simply too decent, and before Stringer could come up with any other alternative to shooting another man cold in the back, Friendly Frank was out the door.

The elderly barkeep heaved a sigh of relief and slid down Stringer's way to ask what all that tenseness in the air had been occasioned by. Stringer shrugged and said, "It's over and you can make my next one a boilermaker."

The barkeep said, "Coming right up. I can see you're a mite upset about something, son."

"I got a right to feel upset," Stringer said. "That other rascal I was jawing with just now left with his winnings, just as the game was getting interesting."

CHAPTER THREE

They'd changed shifts at the Cheyenne Jail since last he'd been there. So Stringer found himself talking with a new desk sergeant. He waited until Stringer had finished before he yawned and asked, "Do you have a permit for that sidearm, Mister MacKail?"

Stinger blinked in astonishment. "What's that got to do with it? Just about every man in town is packing a gun right now. The one I just told you about was packing two when he told me to get out of town."

The police sergeant shrugged and said, "Since nobody got shot, he might have just been playing Frontier Days like everyone else. We ain't got no Friendly Frank Folsom on our yellow sheets. So he likely made that up to go with his cap pistols. That pistol you have on is real. And I can see real bullets in the ammo loops of that gun rig. Nobody's allowed to wander about so ferocious in this town, even during Frontier Days, Mister MacKail."

Stringer hauled out his wallet to show off his press credentials and gun permit. "That was issued by a California judge. It don't cut no ice in this state," the Wyoming lawman opined. "But I'll tell you what I'll do, seeing as I was brung up Christian. You just empty that .38 and take all them other rounds out of your ammo loops and we'll call it playacting for the Frontier Days, hear?"

Stringer stared down at him dumbfounded and protested, "Are you loco? Drunks are shooting live rounds at light bulbs all over town right now and I just told you someone a lot more serious seems to be trying to run me out of town!"

The sergeant yawned and pushed some papers around his desk. "Well, there's a westbound U.P. passing through around midnight and an eastbound even earlier. Whether you want to go or stay is up to you, of course. But, either way, you're going to have to surrender or empty that gun if you don't aim to spend the rest of the night in jail. We don't hold with armed and dangerous drunks in our fair city of Cheyenne."

"Oh, for God's sake, who says I'm drunk, Sergeant?"

"You, for openers. Nobody asked you to come in here with malt liquor on your breath and a wild story of an almost shoot-out at a respectable hotel, you know."

Stringer took a deep breath and let it half out so that his voice might sound reasonable as he explained again, "I had to come here because the U.S. Marshal's office here in Cheyenne has closed for the night. Whether you believe me or not, I feel it my duty to tell Marshal LeFors or *some* damned lawman that some damned body seems to be upset about me talking to Tom Horn this evening."

The desk sergeant looked sincerely puzzled. "Now what could poor old Tom, back in the cell block safe and sound, have to do with your tale of woe and a mysterious two-gun man at your hotel, Mister MacKail?" he asked.

Stringer's patience was wearing thin fast. "He said I'd annoyed someone hereabouts by being nosy. I've only been in town a few hours. So far, I've had a conversation with

STRINGER AND THE HANGMAN'S RODEO   31

Tom Horn and fooled around with the boys over at the fair grounds. Add it up."

The desk sergeant pretended to at least, then said, "There ain't nothing Tom Horn could have told you that the rest of us don't know. How do you know someone else don't have a more reasonable bone to pick with you?"

Stringer was fair-minded enough to consider that before he replied, "The only possible enemies I could have made here in Cheyenne—since I'm new in town—just don't strike me as gents who'd have the wherewithall to hire professional gunslicks, and I'm telling you Friendly Frank struck me as the real thing. He wasn't even mad at me. He came across as a gent who was doing his job, and he backed off just as detached when he decided they might not have been paying him enough for the chore. Maybe if I was to have another interview with Tom Horn..."

"You can't," the desk sergeant cut in, adding, "We run this jail house professional, too. There's other men locked up in the back and they got a right to sleep undisturbed after sundown."

Stringer shot a glance at the wall clock above the officious bastard's head. "It's barely after ten and, no offense, if you listen sharp you can hear a harmonica playing somewhere in the back," he said.

The desk sergeant shrugged again and said, "That would be an old boy we're fixing to hang alongside Tom Horn. Don't he play nice? I wish he knew more tunes, though. I'm still waiting for you to hand over them bullets or tell me you'd enjoy spending the rest of the night listening to harmonica music."

Stringer put his wallet away and proceeded to thumb rounds out of his gun rig as he muttered, "I knew I shouldn't have come here. Maybe I can get Marshal LeFors to pay more attention in the morning."

The desk sergeant chuckled fondly. "I doubts that. Old Joe LeFors is over in the Hole In The Wall Country right now with the posse he's leading to round up the Wild Bunch."

Stringer sighed. "Just my luck. But no doubt I'll be able to talk to one of his deputies at his office, right?"

The desk sergeant produced an empty cigar box for the surrendered rounds. "Wrong. LeFors ain't the marshal here, even when he ain't out after Butch and Sundance. His regular post is Omaha."

"Oh, hell, you mean he got transferred after he arrested Tom Horn?"

"Not hardly. He was kind enough to bring the rascal back here to Wyoming because Wyoming is where Horn done the deed. The U.S. marshals in these parts had nothing to do with the case. You still want to talk to 'em about Tom Horn?"

Having emptied his belt loops, Stringer broke open his .38 to empty that as well into the cigar box as he growled, "I'm going to have to talk to someone, sooner or later, who gives a damn. I hope you know the fix this will leave me in if I run into someone like Friendly Frank when I leave here."

The desk sergeant closed the cover of the box and shoved it in a drawer as he smiled thinly and said, "I think that eastbound pulls in around eleven-fifteen, if waiting on the midnight westbound makes you nervous. I hope you understand that if you pick up some more live ammo after you leave here, we might not be as easy going next time?"

The alley behind the jail house was almost pitch dark and, better yet, someone had parked a Panard two-seater under Tom Horn's tiny window-grid. Stringer climbed up on the driver's seat and whistled through the bars. He only had to do it once before the older man replied, "Who's out there and how come?"

Stringer identified himself and added, "Keep it down.

They wouldn't let me visit you again, and I've got some more to ask you."

Horn said, "Ask away, then. How come I can hear you so good?"

When Stringer explained he was perched on the seat of a horseless carriage, Horn said, *"Bueno.* See if you can find a place to tie one end of this rope I got in here and maybe we can jerk this grid out with all that horsepower."

Stringer said, "I'm not here to bust you out of jail, and even if I was, there'd be no way to start this thing up without the key. Does the name Friendly Frank Folsom mean anything to you?"

Horn replied, "Can't say as it does. What was that about a key, pard? I thought you just got in the fool things and drove off natural, save for not needing a horse, of course. We're talking about a *hanging* here, old son."

Stringer said, "I know. But I don't think the rascals after me could be worried about me helping the state of Wyoming hang you. So let's try her the other way. The gunslick they sent after me let slip that I was nosing into matters they didn't want me to. You're the only mysterious cuss I've had words with that they might have cause to worry about. So what do you reckon they're afraid you might have told me, Tom?"

The prisoner thought some more and decided, "Well, it's no big secret that I'm innocent. I've told everyone who'd listen that I was framed by that two-faced Joe LeFors. If they was pards of mine, fixing to rescue me, they'd be doing that about now, instead of trying to run newspapermen out of town for no sensible reason me and mine might have."

"What if we're talking about someone who wants to make sure you hang, Tom?" Stringer asked.

Horn laughed bitterly and replied, "Hell, they'd have no call to go after anyone else. Unless I can prove my innocence, Wyoming is fixing to hang me as high as anyone might want."

Stringer frowned thoughtfully and said, "Try her this way. What if they thought I was out to prove you innocent?"

"I'd sure like that. How do you aim to start?" Horn said.

Stringer sighed and said, "No offense, but up until a mighty short while ago I was sure you were guilty. Run that part about Marshal LeFors framing you past me again, Tom."

Horn explained. "Neither one of us was anywheres near the Iron Mountain range that time someone else gunned young Willie Nickell. The murder scene was scouted by the sheriff of Laramie County, as he had every right to scout it, being it was his jurisdiction. But they never found no sign connecting me nor anyone else to the killing."

"Then how come a federal marshal arrested you for the crime, Tom?" asked Stringer.

"I wish I knowed for sure," Horn replied. "Being federal, old Joe LeFors has jurisdiction just about anywhere he wants it. That's how come he's allowed to chase the Wild Bunch all he likes, way the hell over in the high country. Joe *said,* at my trial, that I boasted of the killing to him whilst I was in my cups."

"Did you, Tom?"

"Lord have mercy, boy, when I'm drinking serious there's just no telling what I might or might not say. For all I know, I might well have bragged I was Czar of all the Russians whilst he kept ordering more drinks for me. If I *did* say I knew beans about the death of Willie Nickells, I was bullshitting him ferocious, and he should have knowed better than to take me so serious. It ain't as if we never got drunk together afore, you know. Me and Joe goes back a ways. I used to work for him as a part-time deputy."

Stringer whistled softly and said, "Now that's starting to

sound interesting indeed, Tom. When did you work for Marshal LeFors and how come he fired you?"

"I disremember the exact year," Horn replied. "It was the time we was after the Wild Bunch and, let's see, I was the one as took Peg Leg Watson, single-handed. I was tracking out ahead and come on old Peg Leg, holed up alone in a mountain cabin. I reckon I was supposed to wait up for the rest of the posse, but it seemed sort of tedious, just setting there ahint a rock with my saddle gun trained on the fool cabin. So I commenced firing and, well, after swapping shots with me a spell, old Peg Leg saw it was no use and I was able to take him alive."

Stringer whistled again and asked, "Did the posse you were scouting for take any other prisoners?"

"Nope," Horn said. "All the others got away. Peg Leg would have, too, had not I been so far out ahead and, to be fair, him having been left ahint with his peg leg. How come we're talking about Peg Leg Watson, son? I don't see what it could have to do with Joe arresting me for killing Willie Nickell."

"You may know more about tracking than you know about human nature, Tom," Stringer told him. "Didn't it ever occur to you that just by taking that outlaw alive, when your overly eager posse leader might have wanted the glory for his own might have put you in bad with LeFors?"

"I reckon he must have been sore at me about something when he arrested me. But I always thought a man wearing a deputy badge was supposed to go out and *catch* somebody for the law. Didn't you?" Horn sighed.

Stringer frowned. "The world's not as simple as you and I might like it to be, Tom. Did LeFors fire you for making him look less than heroic that time?"

"Nope. He said I'd done right on that job. He never exactly fired me. Like I said, I was working part-time, when they needed extra posse hands, and when I asked how come they never called on me no more, Joe said it was on account of my drinking habits."

Stringer swore softly, then asked, "All right, let's get that out of the way. *Do* you have a drinking problem, Tom?"

Horn sighed and answered, "Not while I'm locked up like this. Even when I'm running loose, I can go weeks at a time without getting in trouble with red-eye. But, yeah, once I do get to drinking I just can't stop and, even worse, I have to allow I'm a sort of mean drunk."

Stringer was about to ask whether the older man remembered what he might or might not have done during one of his drunken episodes. But then someone else was shouting, "What's going on back here?" and as a flashlight beam swept his way Stringer was over the dashboard and rolling under the parked Panard.

It seemed he got to lay there for a million years, listening to the approaching boot heels as the big puddle of flashlight swept closer and closer. Finally, the man holding it stopped, close enough for Stringer to reach out and shine his boots, had he felt so inclined. But the copper badge had his light trained up on Tom Horn's window now as he repeated, "What's going on back here, Tom Horn? Who were you just talking to?"

Considering how slow the older man could seem about some things, he was quick-witted enough to reply, "I was just singing. I got tired of hearing that damned old harmonica across the way and decided to sing me some more interesting songs."

Then, suiting action to his words, Tom Horn proceeded to sing, or croak, "I went down to the cellar, to get a jug of cider/ Where I spied two bedbugs, jerking off a spider/ Come and tie my pecker to a tree, to a tree/ Come and tie my pecker to a tree!"

The copper badge yelled, "Cut that out. You're disgusting. Who owns this horseless carriage here?"

"Is there such a creation out there?" Horn replied. "Oh, yeah, I did hear funny noises out there a spell back. Thought someone was popping corn. What kind of a rig is it?"

The copper badge answered, "Never you mind. You ain't about to go for a spin in it. I want you to cut that coyote yapping, too. Even if you didn't sing so dirty, it's getting late and other folks has a right to sleep. I wonder who owns this here rig."

Tom Horn replied by singing, "Come and set by my side, little darling / Come and tell me how good you can screw."

The law yelled, "Cut that out! I *mean* it!"

"What are you fixing to do if I don't, hang me?"

So the copper badge yelled, "That does it!" and lit out to circle around to the front entrance, giving Stringer the chance to roll out from under the Panard and make tracks the other way.

He stopped running when he came to a side street lined with warehouses and few street lamps. He hoped the older man he'd been talking to would be able to talk himself out of a beating once he shut up, back there.

But as he made his way back to the neighborhood of his hotel Stringer reflected that his own chances didn't look too bright right now. Unless he meant to hop a train out, he'd better pick up some more ammo before he ran into Friendly Frank again. But if the local copper badges caught him packing a loaded gun without a Wyoming permit, he'd be in almost as much trouble.

He stopped to build a smoke in a dark doorway as he muttered half aloud, "Damn it, Boss, you told me covering this wild west show in Cheyenne would be a snap, not the real thing!"

* * *

Stringer gulped when he saw who'd opened the door he'd just knocked on, expecting a man to open up for him. The shapely ash blonde standing there with her hair unpinned for the night must not have known the lamp light behind her was shining through her thin beige kimono so brightly. She just stared up at him with a curious smile. He gulped again and said, "Uh, they told me at my hotel that I'd find the nearest good lawyer, here, ma'am. I know it's late, but would lawyer Morrison, Pat Morrison, be here?"

She replied, "That's me. The first name is Patricia and these are hardly my business hours. But if it's important . . ."

"You might call it a matter of life and death, ma'am," Stringer said. She told him to come on in.

He couldn't see through her kimono once they were on the far side of the floor lamp near the door. But it was still sort of thin and he had to admire the way she walked ahead of him, even though such matters were the last thing for a man to have on his mind right now. She led him out of the little waiting room she had set up, and when they wound up in a smaller office with yet another electrified lamp over a big old desk, she waved him to a leather chair on one side and sat down on the other. She slid open a drawer and got out a pad of yellow ruled paper. Then she picked up a yellow pencil and said, "We usually start with a client's name."

So Stringer told her who he was and that the *San Francisco Sun* would be paying if she billed them sensible. She said she charged five dollars a visit and a dollar an hour in court. Sounded reasonable, he said, so they got down to cases.

From time to time she cut in to clear up a point in his story and he noticed she wrote down only names, times, and places. As he brought her up to date on his recent misadventures Stringer found it sounded sort of wild to him as well. But she never even raised an eyebrow while she heard him out. It made him feel better about her. At second glance, she seemed older and more experienced than he'd taken her for at first sight. He figured her for about thirty-odd, and the framed diplomas hanging on her wall above her blond head allowed she'd been to all sorts of law schools. It wouldn't have been polite to ask why in thunder a woman wanted to be a lawyer. He knew what she was doing in Wyoming. Folk with professional skills were harder to find in cow country, and Wyoming men admired any kind of female so much that they were talking about giving women the vote. A man had to take such political bull with a grain of salt, of course. But it seemed if any states at all ever let the poor sweet things vote, Wyoming would be one of the first.

He was dying for a smoke but knew better than to light up without a lady's permit. So he began to like her even more when they were getting near the end and she took out a pack of tailor-made cigarettes. It was a good thing she smoked them in a long ivory holder. It gave Stringer time to come unstuck and reach across the desk to light her up.

She thanked him and leaned back in her own chair, inhaling thoughtfully as he got down to the part about asking at the hotel about lawyers. He said, "That's about all I know, and does Bull Durham tobacco offend you, ma'am?"

"Oh, I'm sorry," she said quickly, sitting up. "I've been so interested in your story that I fear I forgot my manners." Then she slid the pack of tailor-mades his way. He had to be polite, too, so he took one out and gingerly lit it. It wasn't bad. Just a mite weak. He told her he'd seen the brand advertised on many a barn and that he admired Miss Fatima, whoever she was, for making such nice smokes.

Lawyer Morrison said, "Let's get back to more pressing problems, Mister MacKail. Since my first duty to a client is to give the advice that would probably cost the least bother and expense, there is that midnight train to consider, you know."

Stringer shook his head and said adamantly, "I didn't need a lawyer to tell me leaving town was safe and sure. I'm not trying to be a hero or prove my manhood, either. I've walked out of many a bar fight in my time, and so far, no hair's fallen out of my fool chest. I can't leave because I have a job to do here in Cheyenne. It's as simple as that."

She nodded, blew a thoughtful smoke ring, and said, "You have as much right to attend the rodeo as anyone else I can think of, and it's not as if we're talking about a secret rite. They're expecting a crowd of several thousand."

"I don't think they could be worried about me reporting a calf for cheating in the roping contests, ma'am. They seem to fear I'm interested in raking up that killing Tom Horn was convicted for."

"Convicted and appealed, you mean," she sighed. "I'm not too familiar with the case. But naturally, practicing law here in Cheyenne, one hears things around the courthouse. *Are* you planning to write some sort of exposé about the Nickell killing, Mister MacKail?"

He shook his head. "I don't know a thing about it that hasn't been presented in open court. But, of course, the gents who sent that gunslick after me might not know that."

She made a note, then looked him straight in the eye. "It's obvious they were afraid you were interested in something more important than a calf roping contest." She hesitated a moment. "Let me see if I can't word it another way. As I read it, your life has been threatened, you can't get the local law to take the threat seriously, and you still want to stay here over the weekend. I was married to your breed of man one time. He died in the war with Spain. I couldn't get him to listen to me, either."

She grimaced and added, "Yellowjack. He said he had a job to do. He died without ever getting to the front."

Stringer nodded soberly and said, "I did. He didn't miss much. We lost maybe three or four hundred men in the fighting and over a thousand to Yellowjack. I wrote about that. Nobody wanted to print it. I'm sorry about your man, ma'am. But I still need a gun permit."

She blinked and asked, "Is *that* why you came to me tonight? I thought you were seeking sensible legal advice."

"I knew right after I talked to Friendly Frank that the most sensible thing to do would involve that midnight train. But I was sent here to write a news feature and so I need a Wyoming gun permit if I'm to stay alive until your Frontier Days wind down."

She sighed and, "I told you I'd met your breed of man before. I can probably get a judge I'm on good terms with to issue you a special permit and a restraining order if you feel the police are going out of their way to annoy you."

"I'd like that," he said, nodding. "I could have just run into a natural pain. We had sergeants like that in the army. But it did cross my mind he was being mighty picky about guns at a time when shoe clerks and even some gals seem allowed to be packing 'em, no offense. How early in the morning does this judge of yours open for business?"

She frowned thoughtfully. "Judge Kenton isn't mine or anyone else's. That's why he's the man we want to take your problem too. He's usually in his chambers at the courthouse by nine. But I just remembered he's agreed to act as one of the judges at the rodeo. Hmmm, that could be a problem. We don't want you chasing all over town with that empty gun and he's going to want to see you personally before he issues you any permits."

"They won't be starting the show at the fair grounds until around noon, if that early," Stringer said.

"Judge Kenton will surely want to get there well before the general public is admitted. Could you get us on the grounds before the gates open?"

Stringer nodded. "Sure. I have a press pass, and even better, I know some of the contestants."

She rose from behind her desk, apparently unaware of how open the top of her kimono was. "All right," she said, "let's say we hit the fair grounds less than an hour before the show starts. That ought to throw anyone who's hunting you off stride. I'll naturally have the legal forms filled out for Judge Kenton to approve and sign. Then you'll be free to cover the show as you intended, loaded gun and all."

"I'll still need bullets," he said, frowning. He thought for a moment. "Hold on, I know a friendly gal with the show who collects guns. I'm sure she'll sell me a box of .38s if I ask polite."

"I thought you just told me you had no friends to turn to in this town."

"I don't have, smart as you. Rimfire Rowena is just a sort of good old boy who happens to be a woman. I don't know her well enough to ask for bullets free, if that's what you're interested in."

The lady lawyer raised one cool ash blond eyebrow, then shrugged. "I don't consider the private life of anyone named Rimfire Rowena any business of mine. Once I get you your gun permit, you're free to ask your little cowgirl for bullets or anything else she may have to offer."

"Bueno. What time in the morning do you want me back here to go see that judge?" he asked.

She hesitated. "At the rate you're going, you're more likely to wind up with an interesting obituary than a newspaper scoop. Hasn't it occurred to you that if they sent a man to threaten you at your hotel, they just might know where it is?"

"I hadn't gotten around to where I was planning to spend the rest of the night," he replied. "You're right. I'd better leave my possibles at the Drover's Palace to defend themselves as best they can and scout me up another hotel."

"That's assuming you last long enough to find shelter with an empty gun, what with the crowds thinning away on the dark streets outside—even as we talk about the odds."

"You sure know how to cheer a man who has to walk home in the dark," he said, smiling thinly. "But I don't see how even the Wild Bunch entire could have every street corner in a town this size covered."

"How do you know you weren't followed here from your hotel?" she asked.

"Yeah," Stringer laughed. "You're a regular eternal optimist. I don't suppose you'd have a back door to this layout?"

She beckoned him to follow as she led the way through the side door of her office. Her private quarters were dark. They made it through another doorway and then she switched on one of those fancy Tiffany lamps. He'd expected to wind up in somewhere along the lines of a kitchen, since that was where most folk kept their back doors. But they seemed to be in a bedroom. A lady's magazine lay face down, open, atop rumpled satin sheets, showing what she'd been up to when he came pounding on her front door.

"Good thinking," he said, seeing the open window with the lace curtain blowing from the breeze. "Back doors are easy to cover as front doors. But they might not be expecting anyone to drop out a side window betwixt buildings."

"Oh, for God's sake, to go where, you idiot?" she said as she sat down on the bed and kicked off her silk slippers.

He started to say he recalled a flop house near the depot he could likely make via a back alley. Then, as they locked eyes he wondered why any man would want to say a fool thing like that. But as he took a hesitant step toward her he smiled down at her uncertainly and said what was on his mind. "I sure hope I'm not reading the smoke signals in those big blue eyes wrong, ma'am. For if I am, aside from feeling foolish, I'm likely to hurt like hell."

Her big blue eyes were staring up at him sort of wet and dreamy as she reached to trim her bed lamp, letting her kimono fall open all the way as she replied in a surprisingly pragmatic tone, "Oh, for God's sake, take off your clothes and get in bed with me, you fool. It's my duty to a client to keep you alive. And after all, I told you how well I know your breed of man. That stupid war has been over for quite a spell."

CHAPTER FOUR

By the time they'd gotten past the first awkwardness and were going at it like old pals, Stringer found it somewhat hard to believe Pat had been celibate since her husband had bought the farm in Cuba. She enjoyed it too much and did it too fine for a gal who didn't practice at all. On the other hand, she wept and swore too hard while climaxing for him to worry about a regular lover walking in on them at a time like this.

But just the same, as she lay sprawled and sated for the moment across the now really rumpled sheets, he got up to check both the front and back ways in. Both doors were securely locked with dead bolts nobody was about to get through without waking the dead. So he went back to see if Pat was still alive.

As he rejoined her in bed Pat sniffed, "I'm so glad to see you trust me. Did you really think a law school graduate would be dumb enough to commit adultery on her own premises?"

He put a soothing arm around her naked shoulders and

hugged her mussed-up blond head to his bare chest. "I wasn't worried about friends of yours," he assured her. "I was thinking about enemies of mine. I thought that was the whole point of your kind offer to hide me out here overnight."

"Pooh, there went my chance to be an evil temptress, luring unsuspecting men to their doom."

He kissed the part in her blond hair and told her, "Oh, I suspected you before I got here. That's why I chose your name at random from the city directory they offered me at the Drover's Palace. I figured if a lawyer chosen at random was in cahoots with Friendly Frank, there'd have been no sense in coming after me to begin with. A mastermind big enough to buy even half the lawyers in a town this size wouldn't need hired guns. He'd just put me in jail along with Tom Horn, see?"

"Oh, gee, there goes all my ulterior motives," she said, nibbling on his ear. "Now you'll only remember me as a silly hard-up widow-woman, huh?"

"Yeah, but fondly. Feeling sort of silly beats feeling hard-up by miles—as I hope we both just proved."

"If you have to *ask* whether I came, too, you weren't paying much attention. Are you up to getting sort of silly again, dear?" she giggled.

"In a minute," he said. "Let me get my second wind and it's only fair to warn you that you're in for a mighty silly night. Meanwhile, tell me some more about that judge you'll be taking me to if we survive the night."

"There's no mystery about Judge Kenton, dear. He's a fine old gent, and since I've argued many a case before him, I can say he's a straight shooter. Why do you ask?"

"I'm not sure. I may be on the prod to the point of crazy. On the other hand, they say a man is never more sane than right after he's enjoyed a great lay and has his thoughts sorted out more logical than usual. Would your Judge Kenton have been the judge who heard the case of Tom Horn?"

"Good grief, give me credit for more brains than that!" she sniffed. "You *told* me you suspected someone was after you to keep you from poking into that case. So, even though I know those judges, and can't find anything bad to say about them, I naturally picked a city magistrate who had nothing to do with Mister Horn's state trial. I don't think you're sane enough yet, dear. You just said it hardly seemed likely the entire legal system in these parts could be on one man's payroll."

He rolled her on her back and kissed her. But as he was about to enter her again he said, "Hold on. How come Tom Horn had judges, in the *plural*—not just the usual judge and jury?"

"Silly," she said laughing, "that mean old drunk has had more than one trial since he murdered that boy nearly two full years ago. He keeps appealing, claiming to have new evidence. But, of course, they keep convicting him because he hasn't got any. Do you want me to get on top, if you mean to study law for a spell?"

He laughed, made her gasp in mingled shock and admiration as he drove it in her to the hilt, and they both forgot Tom Horn and everyone else but themselves for a sweet tender time.

There seemed to be just no end to Lawyer Morrison's cleverness. After serving him a fine breakfast in bed, with her for dessert, Pat bathed, dressed, and left him soaking in her tub with orders not to even go near the windows until she got back. It was a lot more restful soaking in that tub without her in it with him, Stringer mused. But after a while the water got cold. So he got out and dressed as well.

He was working on his second Bull Durham in preference to the tasteless tailor-mades she'd left him when she rapped on the back door he'd locked behind her. As he opened it she told him fast, "Come on. There's nobody out back. I made sure." So he grabbed his hat from the kitchen table and followed her across her kitchen garden to the fenced-in alley. There, he stared in wonder at the tall black contraption parked by her back gate. It looked as if someone had crunched a hearse to about a third of its length, and it was hard to say which way the thing was aimed. The front and back looked just the same. "Get in," Pat said. "Nobody is likely to recognize you behind the tinted glass if you sort of lean back."

He climbed in. He knew better than to ask where the horses were. But no motor seemed to be running and she looked sort of skinny to crank the whatever herself. But she just climbed in after him, taking the other seat, facing his as if they were in a pint-sized Concord coach. Then she grabbed hold of something like a bicycle handle stuck to the far side between them, and the next thing Stringer knew he was riding backwards down the alley in an eerie silence.

He laughed. "This thing sure rolls comfortable, in its own spooky way. What in thunder is it?"

She said, "It's a Baker Electric. I have to keep it at a garage a few blocks away because the batteries have to stay plugged in to a special charger when I'm not using it."

He said he imagined it cost her a pretty penny and asked how come she drove it sitting on the back seat instead of up front like everyone else. She told him it had been given to her by a client in payment for a handsome legal fee and that she'd never figured out whether she was driving it forwards sitting in the back seat or backwards sitting in the front seat. And since it seemed to run as good either way, she'd just had to make a choice.

Naturally, it took them no time to get over to the fair grounds, and since nobody seemed to be guarding the gates that early in the day, they just drove on in and rolled along the tanbark until Pat spotted some gents gathered atop a flag-draped box at one end of the bleachers. They rolled to a stop in front of them.

Naturally, everyone in sight was staring at them as Stringer helped Pat down from her amazing rig. A couple of riders were even headed across the tanbark from the far side, chaps flapping and hats respectfully doffed.

Pat yoo-hooed at a portly old gray-haired gent up in the box, and he took his hat off as well. Stringer could tell it wasn't his regular hat. Most of him was dressed in a sedate gray business suit that just didn't go with a ten-gallon snow-white Stetson. Pat told Stringer that was Judge Kenton. Stringer said he never would have guessed and helped her up the pine steps they found at one end of the temporary judges' stand.

At closer range, even with that foolish hat back on, Judge Kenton looked to be a dignified old man with a friendly smile and a firm shake. When Pat told him they'd hunted him down to talk some law with him, the judge led them up into the empty bleachers where they could talk in private. Nobody else seemed to care. Stringer was keeping an eye on everyone in sight, now that he'd been forced to break cover.

He remained standing as Pat and the judge sat side by side on the pine plank benching. Pat took the papers she'd typed up that morning from the briefcase in her lap as she quickly explained Stringer's problem in long Latin-sounding words that no doubt saved time if only one could follow them. After the dumb conversation at the Cheyenne

Jail the night before, Stringer was braced for more of the same. But the kindly old judge just looked up, sort of puzzled, and said, "I don't see why your client has to apply for a gun permit to begin with, Patricia. That city ordinance has been suspended during Frontier Days and half the drunks in town are running around armed and dangerous."

"That's the way it struck me, too, your honor," Pat said. "That's why I'd like you to sign this restraining order for my client as well. It's possible the whole matter simply involves one rather stupid police sergeant. But if it should turn out to be police harassment..."

"Let's see if this fountain pen works," the judge cut in as he reached for the sheaf of papers, adding, "I hope you put an *X* where I'm supposed to sign."

Pat dimpled and said, "I sure did, your honor. But don't you want to read them first?"

Judge Kenton winked up at Stringer and said, "This sweet child has never failed to cross a *T* or dot an *I* in living memory. I only wish half the men practicing law in this town knew half as much about pro forma. How'd you find her, son?"

Stringer grinned down at them both. "Just lucky, I reckon. I'd say she knows how to pick her judges, too, sir."

The older man lowered the broad brim of his big hat to sign Pat's forms wherever she'd inked an *X,* saying, "You're too kind. I can't see a judge or lawyer in Cheyenne arguing that you might not have the right to carry a sidearm during Frontier Days. As to this 'Show Cause', asking the police to leave you alone unless they can prove you're doing something awful, it won't hurt if they're not really out to pester you and it ought to make 'em stop if they are. Who do you suspect could be behind such an unusual police policy, Mister MacKail?"

"I can't say, sir," Stringer said. "Like Pat says, I could have just bumped noses with a desk sergeant who thought I reminded him of a brother-in-law. I had no trouble with anyone the first time I paid a call on old Tom Horn."

The judge looked up with a curious smile. "What on earth would a newspaperman want with Tom Horn at this late date? That case has been raked over the coals every which way since Horn shot that young sheepherder a couple of summers back."

"Tom Horn claims he was framed for a killing he knew nothing about," Stringer explained. "I'd expect him to say that, in any case. But I couldn't help noticing a few loose ends my rival reporters seem to have missed, and, well, if someone wasn't worrying over what else Tom Horn might have told me, we wouldn't be having this conversation."

Judge Kenton pursed his lips. "Hmmm, that case did raise quite a stir and people in these parts are still arguing about it, both ways. Half the locals seem sure Tom Horn is, or was, a vicious killer who deserves to hang whether he murdered that one sheepherder or not. But just about as many feel he was an old hero who at worse shot the wrong sheepherder by mistake. Both his friends and enemies agree he never made much sense when he was drunk."

"He was sober," Stringer said, "both times I talked to him. Do you know anything about his real enemy, Marshal LeFors, sir?"

"Deputy marshal, you mean," replied Kenton. "LeFors is a special deputy, working out of Omaha, mostly with the considerable approval of the Union Pacific, headquartered in Omaha as well. I understand the railroad's provided him with his own private cars to roam their tracks with his posse and their mounts, lest the Wild Bunch stop the U.P. Flier again."

"He seems to have thought that gave him the jurisdiction in the Nickell murder," Stringer said. "Did it, your honor?"

"Any federal peace officer has the right to arrest any criminal, anywhere." The older man frowned thoughtfully. "If you're asking whether that killing was a state or federal crime, it was state. The Nickell boy was killed right here in Laramie County. That's why Tom Horn stood trial for it here in Cheyenne. Deputy Marshal LeFors naturally turned his prisoner and the evidence against him over to Laramie County to be tried and convicted, more than once."

"That is," Stringer insisted, "after said county's sheriff had given up on the case. I can't help finding it odd that a lawman who never investigated the murder scene was able to pin it on a man no witnesses saw anywhere near that boy the morning he died."

Judge Kenton put his pen away as he mused, half to himself, "I don't know Joe LeFors too well. Only met him around the court house a few times. I can't say I enjoyed the experience. He's a sort of pushy gent who admires himself a lot and lets it show. Some go farther, and would have it LeFors has a sinister past as a hired gun. But that may just be jealous gossip and I can't say the man's ever been caught abusing his badge."

"Tom Horn says LeFors was jealous of him," Stringer added, "for showing him up one time."

"He could be grasping at straws, too. I know *I* would."

"So would I, sir. The point is that Tom Horn was convicted on the testimony of a man who, whether he hated Horn or wanted to sit in his lap, had no other evidence to present in court but his own word that an old drinking buddy had confessed the crime to him."

The judge's eyes looked a little glassy in the stark sunlight. "Hmmm, I'd have to go over the transcripts of the trial to be sure there wasn't more to it than that. But you do raise some interesting questions, and if a man wanted to run for governor of Wyoming some day, he couldn't start better than by clearing a man half the state insists could be innocent."

The judge turned to Pat. "Patricia, how long would it take you to draw up papers making Mister MacKail here an officer of my court?"

"I'm a fast typist, your honor. But are we talking officer or friend of the court?"

"You tell me, child. Which would involve the least fuss?" sighed Judge Kenton.

"Since my client is not a Wyoming resident, it might save time if we appointed him an investigative expert witness acting under your carte blanche to... sort of... see what he can see."

"There you go. Ain't she something?"

"I think so," Stringer said. "What are we talking about, sir?"

Pat explained. "Actually just a writ, signed by his honor, authorizing you to poke your nose anywhere you like without being pestered by petty officious types."

Stringer asked if they meant he'd be some kind of deputy judge and Judge Kenton said that was close enough. So Stringer said, "Hold on. I was sent here to cover this here wild west show."

Judge Kenton shrugged and said, "You can, as a guest in my box if you like. I just thought, since someone keeps telling you not to look any deeper into the case of Tom Horn..."

"I may as well have me a hunting license," Stringer cut in with a grin. "I'd be much obliged, your honor. I can't wait to see what Friendly Frank has to say, if ever we meet up again with bullets in my gun and your paper in my pocket!"

* * *

Pat Morrison gave him the papers the judge had already signed and told him she'd have the rest ready at her office that very afternoon. Then she left him to follow his own way back to the chutes and stock pens.

Stringer found Rimfire Rowena sitting on the tailgate of her gypsy cart, cleaning the .22 repeating rifle in her lap. She looked even prettier in broad daylight. She replied to his polite howdy with, "Who was that brassy blonde you got outten that fancy horseless carriage with just now?"

Stringer chuckled. "I was afraid you hadn't noticed. She ain't a brassy blonde. She's my lawyer. I've only spent the night with her one time."

It worked. Rimfire Rowena cocked her head back and spat, "That'll be the day. I'll bet that dress she was wearing cost fifty dollars and you're too raggedy to court a self-respecting squaw. How come you need a lawyer? Is some she-goat suing you for child support?"

He sighed. "I sure admire a gal who wakes up so cheerful and friendly, Miss Rowena. The reason I needed a lawyer was because a pesky copper badge took all my bullets away from me last night. We got that straightened out. But now I need me at least a box of .38 longs."

She swung her target rifle up to squint through the barrel as she replied, "There must be dozen hardware shops in town that stock pistol rounds."

"I noticed," he said. "Getting that far with my fool gun empty could be a problem, though. I have at least one gent gunning for me, and the last time I saw him, both his guns seemed to be loaded."

She lowered her rifle and looked sincerely concerned. "For heaven's sake, why didn't you say right out that you were in trouble again? How come you get in so many fights to begin with?"

He started to say he was no doubt just lucky. But Rimfire Rowena had already rolled over to crawl into her cart on hands and knees, presenting a rump to him that managed to look naughty as hell, even covered by tanned deerskin. He heard her cussing and fussing inside for a time before she returned, head first, to hand him a greasy pasteboard box. "This is the best I can do you," she said. "They're shorts, and black powder, but they'll fit your S&W, 'til you can find something fancier."

"I didn't know Remington still made black powder .38s. How much do I owe you, Miss Rowena?"

"Don't talk dirty to a lady. I'm a sharpshooter, not a shopkeeper, and they ain't worth much, anyways. You're right about the line being discontinued. I don't know why I hung on to 'em when I swapped my old .38 for a better balanced .32 a spell back. But lucky for you, I'm half pack rat."

He told her she was sure a pretty little rodent and put the box on the tailgate to begin reloading. He picked out the least green shells for his sidearm. As he began to fill the bullet loops of his rig he found himself asking just how long a spell they were talking about, adding, "No offense, but gunpowder more than seven or eight years old ain't too apt to go off."

"I don't reckon it's been seven years," she replied. "Let's see now. I was about sixteen when I got good enough to join the rodeo circuits and I was using that old .38 until I was twenty or more. So they ain't seven years old, quite yet."

He didn't answer. He knew better than to ask a lady her age and he didn't see why she wanted him to add it up in his head. "I reckon you thought I was a heap younger, huh? I reckon you thought I was just a bitty small-town gal. But I guess I've been around, some," she said, answering his unspoken question.

He assured her he could see she was a woman of the world. As he turned to go he ticked his hat to her and told her she was a real pard.

She said, "Hold on. Just let me get that .32 I told you about and I'll go with you."

"Go where, Miss Rowena?" he asked with a puzzled smile.

"I don't know if you don't," she said. "Didn't you say we was fixing to have a show-down with some gunslick?"

"Not hardly. I'm trying not to meet any more Friendly Franks, but even if I do, it'll be a private fight. Boys only," he laughed.

She looked hurt and turned away. He ticked his hat at her again anyway and headed back to civilization. When he was clear of the last chutes he saw Pat had driven off in her Baker Electric. He headed for the nearest exit on the far side, walking catty-corner across the tanbark. He was maybe two hundred feet from the chutes when he heard an angry female voice call out to him and turned to see the distant figure of Rimfire Rowena with a nickel-plated six-gun in one hand. She yelled, "See that horse apple two feet from your boots?" When he looked down, he could indeed see such an object almost at his feet, Rimfire Rowena fired from the hip and pulverized it. Then she turned her back and flounced out of sight.

"Remind me never to get that little sass really upset," Stringer chuckled to himself. Then he headed on back to town.

Stringer doubted Pat would have those other papers ready yet but an established member of the Fourth Estate didn't need a court order to paw through a newspaper morgue.

A staffer who kept calling him "Frisco Boy" led Stringer back to the files and made sure he didn't smoke as he scanned what they had on Tom Horn's case, which included reporter's notes and clippings from other papers as well as what they'd printed themselves. It added up to quite a pile. But Stringer was a fast reader who, like most experienced researchers, could skim over stuff that was repeating what he'd already read whether it was worded just the same or not. So in less than an hour he'd put their file on Tom Horn back together as neatly as he'd found it and slammed the steel drawer shut with a snarl.

His rival newspaper man rose from the steam radiator he'd been perching on to ask with a yawn, "Find what you were looking for?"

"Too much," Stringer answered angrily. "How many versions of that story did you run, anyway?"

The older and more jaded staff writer shrugged. "As many as we could figure out. Next to beef, the main product of cow country would seem to be bullshit. As if Tom Horn being a pathological liar wasn't enough, half the lawmen connected with the case chose to change their original 'Beats Me' to an 'I Knew It All the Time' as the case against Horn developed."

"I read the interview where that posse member suddenly recalled seeing the rock under the dead boy's head, almost a year after they scouted the scene without finding any sign." Stringer grimaced. "I'm just wondering why Tom Horn claims he was riding for Joe LeFors when he captured Peg Leg Watson when the Pinkertons say he was riding for them and that they thought it was Peg Leg McCoy?"

"I can answer part of that," the older man offered. "Watson held up trains under the name McCoy. I think Joe LeFors used to work for Pinkerton as well. *He's* as hard to pin down about his past as Horn. We were even afraid to run one interview we had on the cuss. A local cattle baron with a reputation for paying his bills told one of our reporters that Tom Horn and Joe LeFors had once hung cow thieves for the C.P.A. together, sort of informal."

"Do tell? I didn't find that in your morgue."

"Of course you didn't. We don't like to be sued for libel any more than the fancy *Frisco Sun*. You know how many so-called lawmen started out as law benders in these parts. Good help is hard to find, and it's catching two birds with one stone to hire a worn-out outlaw as a law officer. It gets you a good gunfighter at a moderate salary and often keeps him from holding up any more banks."

As they headed back out front Stringer said, "I dunno. If I had a lick of sense I'd forget the whole thing. Joe LeFors is far away. Tom Horn's in jail, and the case is so old and larded over with contradictions that Sherlock Holmes couldn't make much sense of it."

The staff man walked him to the front door and asked where Stringer aimed to go next.

"Back to the fair grounds, I reckon," Stringer said. "That was the story I was sent here to cover in the first damned place. I can't say I enjoy being told to back off any news lead. But the rest of the profession has had a good two years to make some sense of the Nickell killing, and no offense, you can't even make up your mind whether Horn was arrested in Omaha or here in Cheyenne."

The older man laughed and told him that yet another paper had LeFors luring Horn to Montana with a promise of a job before arresting him. The two newsmen agreed it was a pisser and split up.

Stringer stood undecided for a moment on the hot cement walk. It was only a little after high noon. The stands by now would be sun baked and he knew the opening ceremonies involved hours of flag waving, speeches, chuck wagon parades, and such. They hardly got into the interesting events the first day, if at all. So, unless those swinging doors just across the street indicated the entrance of a church, he had plenty of time for a cold beer.

He was halfway across when a husky male voice behind him called out, "Stringer!" He almost changed the future format of many a pulp magazine by blowing away Bat Masterson.

But as he knelt there on the hot asphalt with his gun out and trained he recognized the older gent and fellow newspaperman just in time.

The Canadian-born William Bartholomew Masterson was fifteen or twenty years older than Stringer but still a handsome man who kept in good shape. No doubt he had to, to get away with sporting a derby hat and silver-handled cane in Cheyenne on a day like today. Like Stringer, he was a reliable reporter who called things as they were. But some said he was a more accurate sports reporter than an objective historian of his own early years, or at least one summer, down in Dodge.

As Stringer got back to his feet and holstered his .38 with a sheepish smile, Masterson joined him. "How come you pulled that one on me, MacKail?" Masterson asked mildly, "Didn't your mother ever tell you it's not nice to throw down on kindly old sports reporters? Had you been someone I didn't know, acting so strange, I might have gone for my own pistol, and then where would we have been?"

"Sorry, Bat," Stringer said laughing. "You called me from behind at a bad time. Have you ever heard tell of a gent called Friendly Frank Folsom?"

Masterson shook his head. "He sounds like someone

Ned Buntline made up. I sure miss old Ned. Didn't he tell amazing tales about us whilst he was still alive?"

"Friendly Frank is real," Stringer explained. "So let's take cover in that saloon while I tell you how come I'm so proddy this afternoon. What are you doing here in Cheyenne, Bat?"

"The same as you, I imagine. I came out to cover this fool rodeo as a sporting event. That's what they call it, a sporting event. I don't know about you, but in my salad days I tried to avoid horses that bucked. Now they pay a man good money to ride a bronc we would have just shot as useless when beef was a serious industry."

They went inside. The place was nearly empty at this hour, since just about anyone not tied down to a local job was out at the fair grounds, watching Indian chiefs wave flags en masse.

They both ordered beer and took a corner table. Masterson would have sat with his back to the wall, of course, had not Stringer said, "I've got better call to watch the doorway, if it's all the same to you, Bat."

Masterson shrugged and surrendered the corner to Stringer. "It's been a spell since anyone's tried to creep up behind me," the dapper reporter said. "You're right. You're really on the prod. I used to see that same look in a man's eyes while I was shaving. That's one of the reasons I gave up packing a badge. What's this all about, son?"

Stringer brought his fellow newspaperman up to date on his recent adventures, leaving out the slap and tickle with Pat, and Masterson decided flatly, "Back off, old son. It's not your fight. Joe LeFors and me go back a ways. We ain't enemies. But he ain't the sort of man who collects friends. He's a hard man. The men who ride with him are the same. If any of 'em thought you were out to make a liar of Joe LeFors they wouldn't send a tin horn to scare you.

They'd come after you personal." He inhaled some suds, then added, "As for Tom Horn, I know him of old and he's loco."

"Do you think he gunned that young sheepherder?" Stringer asked.

"I wasn't there," Masterson replied. "All I know about it, aside from what you've just told me, is what I read in the papers back east, and for some reason the *New York Times* didn't carry it on the front page. I'll allow it surprised me to read old Tom had been accused of a cowardly bushwhacking, since it was never his style in the past. If anything, he was always brave to the point of suicidal despair. You know about him and Geronimo, of course?"

"I just read in the morgue across the street that he'd scouted for Miles in that campaign, down Arizona way."

"He did more than scout," Masterson said, wiping the foam from his mouth. "He tracked Geronimo's band down, lonesome. Then he rode into their camp—alone—and told Geronimo, in the flesh, that he was there to take them in peaceable."

Stringer whistled softly. "That sounds like a good way to wind up naked on an ant pile, smeared with honey."

"I told you Horn was crazy. Lucky for him, Geronimo was sane, tired of running, and knew about the mountain artillery Miles was packing with the main column. So in the end Horn arranged an honorable surrender."

"Naturally, the War Department didn't honor the terms and fired Horn as a scout, now that they had no further use for his services." Masterson grimaced. "You might say he talked his fool self out of a job. My point is that he was willing to face Geronimo man-to-man, not shoot him in the back, and Geronimo was not exactly a fourteen-year-old boy, unarmed."

Stringer began to roll a smoke as he tried to recall the

clippings he'd been reading. "One of the more popular theories put forward was that Horn shot the kid in the mistaken belief he was aiming at his father, Kell Nickell."

"In broad daylight, from no more than two hundred yards away, if the killer really did fire from the nearest cover?" Masterson asked. "Not if Horn was half sober. And drunk or sober, he'd have had no reason to fear a trash white homesteader, man or boy. The Tom Horn I know wouldn't have been laying for anyone like that in the first place. He'd have just gone right to their front door and done whatever he'd been sent to do."

"I heard about the way he dealt with an outlaw forted up in a cabin," Stringer said. "Maybe he just didn't want any witnesses, and if he hadn't been paid to murder the whole family..."

"He'd have gunned 'em on the house," Masterson finished, adding, "I never said Tom Horn was *nice*. Just crazy-brave. But, hell, what are we arguing about? The man's had a fair trial, and if they mean to hang him for something he didn't do, it's not as if he never did anything, you know. Look on the bright side and consider all the killing the old coot's gotten away with in his time. I don't see how any man could have managed to kill the forty or so Tom brags on, unless you want to count Indians. But it was his own notion, not yours or mine, to live by the gun, and like I was forced to decide some time ago, that ain't no way to live if a man aims to die of old age."

Stringer fumbled for a match to light his smoke and Masterson instantly reached across the table with a handsome patent lighter, murmuring, half to himself, "It's a shame poor old Tom couldn't quit whilst he was ahead, when the Indian fighting trade got slow. He had the makings of a mighty fine cowhand. He won the roping prizes total at the Globe rodeo a few years back."

Stringer frowned thoughtfully as he got his smoke going, and then, as Masterson put the lighter away he said, "There wasn't anything across the street about winning roping prizes. What year are we talking about, Bat?"

The older reporter shrugged and replied, "Just before Queen Victoria died. I can't recall the exact date. They started all this rodeo bullshit down in Globe in the nineties. I mean, with formal rules and all. Before that it was just cowhands funning around when they had no better chores to tend to. Anyway, they gave Tom Horn a fancy gold-plated belt for being the world's champion roper, they said. So he could have no doubt gotten many an honest job with lots a cattle spread after that. But, like I said, he chose to live by the gun as a half-ass range detective and full-time drunk, and now they're going to hang him and I'd better get on out to the fair grounds and see who's fixing to win the roping contests this year."

"Hold on a minute," Stringer said. "They're still making speeches out there and I may have a deal you'd be interested in, Bat."

Masterson drained the last of his schooner. "I'm listening," he said.

"Look, Bat, I was sent to do a feature on that rodeo, the same as you," Stringer was saying. "At the same time I suspect I may have stumbled over something hotter. But I can't be in two places at one time. So how do you feel about sharing both stories?"

"You mean, if I cover the rodeo for you, you'll give me an exclusive on whatever the hell you think you're working on? I dunno, kid. It's not as if our papers were deadly rivals in the same town, but . . ."

"But me no buts," Stringer cut in, insisting, "You work for a New York paper. I work for a west coast paper.

There's no conflict of interests if we share both stories, is there?"

Masterson stared down wistfully at his empty beer schooner and decided to go for a cigar instead of a second round. As he fished out a Havana Claro, he said, "That's assuming there *is* another story, and that you're content with the way I cover the rodeo for you."

He bit the end off his cigar, spat, and explained, "I wouldn't want this to get around, Stringer. But you just may be a mite more, ah, western than me. I tried to tell my editor that I was never a cowhand in my misspent youth. But you know how good old Ned Buntline carried on about the time I acted as a deputy for my older brother, Ed."

Stringer nodded gravely. "I read about the way they murdered your big brother, all seven versions, and I'm sure sorry about every one of 'em. Bat. But, come on, you were in Dodge at the height of the cattle-driving days."

Masterson lit his cigar with the same fancy machine, then he confessed, "As a part-time lawman and full-time townee, son. I ride pretty good. I shoot pretty good. I've never roped a calf in my life, and as for that bulldogging..."

"Nobody ever did that until a cowboy invented it at a Texas rodeo a year or so ago," Stringer cut in, explaining with a chuckle. "He missed with his rope and, feeling sort of frusterpated, just leaped on the critter and wrestled it to the ground. The judges were so delighted they declared it a new event and awarded him a prize for acting so unusual."

Masterson sucked in some expensive smoke. "I'd say he deserved it. My point is that my reportage of the rodeo here is more likely to be colorful than accurate. When I'm not sure of the finer points of a game I'm covering, I sort of fake it with humorous observations, and to tell the plain truth, I'm not up on the funny rules they have about riding mean horses and such these days."

"Neither are our readers," Stringer soothed him, laughing. "But surely you can tell when a roper misses or a rider gets thrown, can't you?"

"Sure, but I'll be blamed if I can see why the judges give one entrant more points than another when they both do about the same thing from where I'm sitting."

"You don't have to. They announce how many points they're awarding and you just have to write 'em down. All I need to fake my own feature for old Sam Barca is who won what or who got hurt enough to be worth printing. Come on, Bat, you're going to have to take the same notes for your own damned story, aren't you?"

Masterson shrugged. "All right, don't say I never warned you if I get something wrong and we both wind up looking dumb. Where will you be while I'm trying to tell a cowboy from an Indian, MacKail?"

"I thought I'd hire a livery mount and ride over to Iron Mountain, where that boy was murdered. Folk in the neighborhood might be able to sift some wheat from a lot of chaff. It's only a few hours ride, you know."

"A few *hot* hours in the saddle at this time of day, you mean. If I was you," Masterson cautioned, "I'd wait until the prairie sun got a mite lower."

"I might just do that. I have to stop off at my ... ah ... lawyer's place before I leave town. You're damn right about this being an awkward time to ride—a horse, that is." Stringer grinned.

CHAPTER
FIVE

Just where the High Plains of Wyoming met the official foothills of the Laramie Mountains was a matter of opinion. The crossroads hamlet of Iron Mountain lay in what could be called low foothills or mighty rolling prairie, depending on who was calling the shots. Stringer hadn't made his mind up, yet. The wagon trace he was following on a roan livery gelding was undulating up and down across over-grazed and summer-dried shortgrass. But from time to time he passed an outcrop of bare rock, mostly sandstone, and some of the draws were choked with mountain aspen as well as the usual crack willow, chokecherry and cottonwood official to prairie draws.

He'd stayed at Pat's place in Cheyenne a mite longer than he'd intended, so it was a mite cooler than his denim jacket called for when the evening breezes caught him topping a rise. He was just commencing to worry about getting caught by sundown in the middle of nowhere when he topped another rise and spied rooftops and chimney smoke ahead. It had to be Iron Mountain because he'd ridden about five hours and it was about time he got to anyplace.

He rode into town, what there was of it, and dismounted in front of the one combined saloon and general store. As he did so his tired mount tried to inhale all the water in the trough out front at once. He patted its lathered neck. "I'm sorry about that, Red. I tried to tell her I had a long way to ride before that summer sun went down, but would she listen?"

Then he tethered the reins to a handy post and stiff-legged up the plank steps and through the open doorway. At this hour a modest crowd of townees and, judging from their outfits, some hands off surrounding spreads, had gathered to celebrate the end of another hard day's work. There was a hard-eyed but good-looking gal of about twenty-five sitting at a corner table, playing cards with herself. Everyone else was standing at the bar, paying her no mind. From the way she was dressed in that low-cut purple satin outfit, it seemed obvious she wasn't exactly there to play cards. Her black hair was sort of purple at the ends, too. He wondered what color hair she really had. But, like the others, he bellied up to the bar and said he sure could use a boilermaker if they refused to serve him a barrel of ice water.

The friendly fat barkeep laughed, said it was late in summer for ice in those parts, and filled a shot glass and beer mug as he added, "You do look like someone drug you through the keyhole backwards, stranger. How long have you been on the trail?"

Stringer swallowed the contents of the shot glass and half the beer before he gasped, "Oh, that felt good. I just rode up from Cheyenne, faster than I'd planned. Walking my mount up the slopes and loping him down. I'm going to have to oat him and rub him down some before it gets any cooler up this way. Do you sell oats?"

"Right next door," the barkeep said. "Tell my wife I sent you and she won't sell you chicken feed. Are you planning on riding on or staying, stranger?"

"I'll be in town at least overnight," Stringer said, "if I can find shelter for me and a mighty deserving mount. Since I can see I've aroused your curiosity, gents, I'd best tell you I'm called Stringer MacKail and that I write stories for the *San Francisco Sun*. They sent me to these parts to cover the Frontier Days in Cheyenne."

A morose-looking cuss in a black satin shirt and gun-barrel chaps growled, "How come you're *here,* then?"

"I thought as long as I was in the neighborhood, I'd ride up here and see if there was anything new on that killing you had in Iron Mountain a year or so back," Stringer told them.

It got sort of quiet—fast. The fat barkeep politely put a new head on Stringer's beer as he said in a less jolly tone, "Folk in these parts have been trying to forget that old feud, son. Like you said, it was long ago, and they got the man who murdered Willie Nickell."

A cowhand further down muttered, "Or so they say." Then the one in the gunbarrel chaps snapped, "Shut up, Casey. You don't know nothing about it. None of us know nothing about it."

There was an almost ominous growl of agreement the length of the bar. Stringer swallowed some more beer, left his change on the mahogany, and said he might be back after he saw to his mount. As he was leaving, the one in gunbarrel chaps advised him nobody would worry about him if he failed to return.

The motherly woman in the attached general store was much more friendly. So he decided not to mention any local murders to her. She said she'd be proud to sell him a sack of oats and when he asked if there was a livery in town she said, "No, but the blacksmith catty-corner across the way boards horses. I think he asks a dime a day, with you providing feed, I mean."

Stringer said that sounded fair, paid her more than he should have for the oats, then went out to untether his roan and lead it the short way to the open front of the smitty across the way. He found the smith about to close down for the night. But they cut an easy deal and it was still fairly light out by the time his roan was rubbed down and stalled, his saddle tacked, and so on. The smith said he had no idea where Stringer might or might not find a room for himself. He explained he had to share the one bed he had with a lady he meant to marry up with any day now.

So once he found himself alone on the dusty and only street again, Stringer rolled a smoke as he pondered his next move. As a seasoned newspaper man, he'd learned that folks came in just two species: those willing to be interviewed, and those that were possibly dangerous if a stranger kept pestering them. From what he could see of the tiny town in the rapidly fading light of gloaming, it was an even smaller and more tightly knit community than he'd expected. He knew from his earlier reading at the newspaper morgue in Cheyenne that there seemed to be at least two factions, sheep and cow, in these parts, and that things had been mighty tense at the time the son of Kell Nickell, a leader of the sheep men, had been murdered. He could see why the obvious cow men across the street might not want anyone even hinting that an outsider, such as Tom Horn, might not have done the deed. But even if he couldn't get anyone to talk to him, he still needed a place to bed down, damnit, so he lit his smoke and headed toward the lamp light of the saloon again.

STRINGER AND THE HANGMAN'S RODEO 71

But as he did so a female voice hissed, "Don't go back there. Not if you know what's good for you." He spun around to see that, sure enough, the fancy gal he'd seen there before had snuck out to join him.

He smiled down at her curiously and said, "To tell the truth I did detect a certain lack of warmth over yonder, ma'am. But I just hate to spend nights standing out in the cold like this and I can't say any of the boys treated me downright mean."

"A lot you know," she said sarcastically, "if your name is Stringer and you're a newspaperman. If it was, another stranger was in town not two hours ago, asking for you by name and chosen trade."

"Do tell? I wonder how come none of those boys saw fit to tell me a thing like that?"

"I was wondering the same thing. That's why I ducked out to tip you off. Unlike some I know in these parts, I don't like noise. The man who was asking for you earlier struck me as a hired gun."

"Tall gent, in a frock coat and a brace of ivory-gripped guns in a cross-draw rig?" Stringer asked.

She shook her head. "One gun, black grips, worn low and tie-down. He smiled a lot. But I could tell he even had Sweet Violets scared skinny."

He smiled thinly. "Who on earth is Sweet Violets, and by the way, who might you be, ma'am?"

"You can call me Cherokee," she said. "You were talking to Sweet Violets Vance before. He was right next to you in skinny chaps and a Harrington Richardson .44."

"Right. What makes you think they're all in on it, if that other gent was a stranger in town as well?"

"They're not with him. They're not with you. They're just waiting to see who wins so they can root for the winner. I think old Fats, behind the bar, may have sent for the law. He's got more sense than your average cowhand. Meanwhile the nearest deputy lives a good ways out of town and it's an even bet who might get here first. That gunslick never said whether he was leaving for good or just scouting about for his old pal Stringer MacKail. If I were you, I'd be mounted up and going lickety-split about now."

"You ain't me, Cherokee, and my mount is too jaded to go lickety-anything right now," Stringer shrugged.

"All right," she relented, a little too easily. "What say you hole up with me for the night, then?"

He raised an eyebrow and said, "I sure hope you won't take this personal, ma'am. But while I have to say your approach is original as hell, I'm just too romantic by nature to pay my way into any gal's bed."

She gasped. "Oh, you brute, is that any way to talk to a lady?"

"Nope," he replied politely. "But ain't you sort of stretching the definition a mite, Miss Cherokee?"

"You idiot, I'm a card shark, not a whore, and I was only suggesting you'd be safer on my sofa than in that saloon across the way!"

"Sure you were," he retorted, tipping his hat. "It's been nice talking to you, Miss Cherokee. But it didn't work. And now, with your permission, I'll go see if old Fats and his wife purvey any creature comforts besides grain and the spirits derived therefrom."

As he moved on she tagged along, insisting, "You have to believe me. I've been laying in wait here for the Frontier Days in the city to break up. I don't exactly cheat at blackjack but the odds are always with the dealer, and it's my sincere hope some of the hands passing through will have won big at that rodeo, see?"

Stringer said, "A man who'd leap off a pony at a steer would likely bet against a lady with purple hair and it's a free country. But you're just wasting your temptations on *me,* ma'am."

She called him a total fool and dropped back as he got closer to the lamp light. He entered the saloon to announce, "I'm sure sorry to disappoint you, boys. But I said I might be back."

Nobody who'd been there earlier answered. But a gent sporting a red silk shirt and a smile almost as flashy stepped away from the bar to ask, "Would you be Stringer MacKail, little darling?"

Thanks to Cherokee's warning about a holster worn low and tie-down, Stringer beat him to the draw by a split second, and thanks to the black powder shells Rimfire Rowena had given Stringer, the galoot staggered back with three balls in his chest and his fancy shirt on fire.

He landed face up in the sawdust, still smiling and still on fire. The hand called Casey emptied a beer schooner on the dead man's chest and said laconically, "That's ten dollars you owe me, Sweet Violets. I told you a man who goes to so much trouble with his gun rig could be uncertain about the subject."

Sweet Violets growled, "It's the accepted custom to answer a man afore you slap leather on him."

Stringer finished reloading, put his .38 back in its holster, and turned to face Sweet Violets as he inquired mildly, "Did you say something, Sonny?"

Sweet Violets didn't answer. Another hand laughed jeeringly and said, "Say something to the man, Sonny."

"Aw, shut up," Sweet Violets said. "It ain't my fight and the law is already going to have a lot to say about the one man down already."

As if to prove his words, an older gent covered with trail dust burst through the doorway with the young hand Fats had sent to fetch him legging right behind. They both had their guns out. The older one stared morosely down at the smouldering cadaver on the floor and said, "Well, I tried to get here in time. What's this all about, Fats?"

"The dead man was in earlier, looking for that stranger in blue denim," the barkeep said. "When they finally met just now, the results was what you see, Deputy."

The lawman didn't exactly point his Dragoon .45 at Stringer. But he didn't put it away either as he asked, "Which one was first to go for his gun, Fats?"

The barkeep answered, "Hard to say. From where I stood it looked like a meeting of the minds. The dead man did call MacKail first, and he'd been sort of hinting at death and destruction earlier."

Casey said, "I was closer. The dead man's mouth and gun hand was moving at the same time. Stringer, there, beat him to the draw fair and square."

The old deputy nodded at Stringer. "Your turn, son."

Stringer said, "I don't have much to add. I never saw the man before. But since it's obvious he was laying for me here, he must have thought he was following me up from Cheyenne and got here sooner. I left Cheyenne a little later than I'd planned this afternoon. I'm still working on who could have told him I meant to come up here at all."

The local law asked, "Why did you come here in the first place?"

So Stringer said, "With your permission, I mean to reach under this jacket for some papers that may explain me better to you."

As Stringer did so Sweet Violets said, "Watch him, Jim. He moves quick as a cat." But the old-timer was already covering Stringer pretty good as he hauled out the papers Pat Morrison had given him that afternoon with a fond farewell kiss.

The deputy moved over to spread them atop the bar

under the better light there as the young hand who'd fetched him continued to smile politely or perhaps bemusingly at Stringer, gun in hand. The old-timer read everything twice before he decided, "Well, I savvy this permit to pack a gun in Wyoming, even though I never knew you needed one. I don't understand this court order telling the Cheyenne P.D. to stop pestering you, though. Was that man you just gunned a Cheyenne copper badge? He don't look like one."

"I don't know who he was," Stringer insisted. "Read the writ appointing me a friend of the court and authorizing me to look into the murder of Willie Nickell."

Some of the others sucked in their breath and one said softly, "Oh, shit, not that again!"

The old deputy said, "I already read it. Like I said, it's all mighty confusing. But if a county judge says it's all right for you to snoop about I don't see how the sheriff's department can stop you. I don't see nothing here giving you the right to shoot nobody in my jurisdiction, though."

Stringer said, "I thought anybody had the right to defend himself. The jasper came after me. I never went after him."

The older man handed the papers back to Stringer, glanced down at the dead man again, then said, "It appears to me he might not have known exactly what he was looking for. For openers, I'd best see if I can find out who in thunder he might have been. Meanwhile, you wasn't planning on leaving town in the near future, was you, Mister MacKail?"

Stringer said, "Well, I meant to spend at least tonight and the better part of tomorrow poking about in these parts. I have to be back in Cheyenne before that rodeo winds down, though."

The old deputy shook his head wearily and said, "I'm

not so sure about that. I'll take your word you gunned that other gent in self-defense. I'd have to lock you up if I didn't. But even when a man has witnesses, we do things tidy here in Iron Mountain. Our assistant county coroner is surely going to want you to appear afore his panel, and with the weekend coming up and Doc Marvin out of town in any case, there's just no saying when they'll be able to get around to it."

Stringer swore softly and asked, "Why can't you report it to the county coroner, direct, so I can appear before him down in Cheyenne?"

The old man moved past him to hunker over the corpse as he told Stringer, "I could. I don't aim to. Doc Marvin would never forgive me if I was to spoil his chances to hold a proper hearing. Doc takes his position serious and we hardly ever get such an interesting death for him to investigate."

The old lawman spit on his palm to pat out some threads still smouldering on the dead man's chest as he muttered, "Must be that fake silk they make outten cotton and lye water. Do you reckon he come to Cheyenne to ride in the rodeo and then got side-tracked?"

"That should be easy to check by wire, if you have a telegraph office here," Stringer said. "I know a judge who's with the rodeo committee."

Old Jim said, "We can do better than Western Union. We got us a telephone line to Cheyenne now. I told you we do things right here in Iron Mountain. But first we got to figure out who the poor son of a bitch was."

He rolled the cadaver over to go through its hip pockets and sure enough produced a wallet. He opened it, slid out a voter's registration card, and announced, "Winfield Scott Rutherford from Hayes, Kansas, it says here. Have any of you boys ever heard tell of such a gent?"

Nobody had. Casey opined, "It's likely a fake I.D. I knowed he was somebody sinister the moment he first walked through the door."

Old Jim shrugged and said, "At least it's a name to start with. There's no sense pestering folk in other parts about him before morning. Everyone who knows his ass from his elbow will have gone home by this hour. He ought to keep overnight if we can find him a cool root cellar. I want you to meet me here right after breakfast, Mister MacKail. Where will you be if I should need you any sooner?"

Stringer said, "That's a good question." Then he turned to Fats to explain, "I came back here to ask if you had a spare room, or knew of one I could hire. What happened then was that other gent's idea."

The fat barkeep looked away and said, "I fear I can't help you with that one, son. Maybe if you asked around town."

Stringer didn't press it. He shrugged and said, "Well, if push comes to shove I reckon I can spread my bedroll on the prairie. I'd best start by picking up said bedroll from the tack room across the way."

Nobody argued. But as he stepped out to the street the friendly hand called Casey caught up with him, moved him out of line from the inside lights, and said, "It ain't that we're usually so unkind to strangers, MacKail. You just never should have mentioned you was interested in that Nickell killing, see?"

Stringer nodded. "I did get the impression it's not a favorite topic of conversation in these parts. But since I rode all this way to talk about it, that's the way it has to be. Which side are you on, Casey?"

The cowhand said flatly, "The living, if I can manage to stay among them. To do that, it's best to stay on good terms with both the Nickells and the Millers. That ain't easy as it sounds. They're both still mighty proddy about the way their feud ended with that child's death. Some say it never really ended it. So it ain't too smart to ask either side, see?"

Stringer started to ask a dumb question. Then he remembered all the reading he'd been doing of late and said, "The Millers were neighbors of the Nickell clan, and not on such good terms with them, right?"

Casey grimaced. "You might say that. Less than six months before Willie Nickell was murdered in the summer of '01, James Miller and Kell Nickell had 'em a free-for-all that brung the neighbors from near and far. It ended with Miller putting his Bowie knife in Kell Nickell and leaving him for dead in the snow. Kell Nickell survived and refused to press charges, intimating he'd handle the son of a bitch his own way once he was up and about again."

"Where does Tom Horn fit in?" Stringer asked.

"You tell me," Casey replied. "Tom Horn was known in these parts as a man whose gun hand could be rented by the hour, at a higher price than either of them trash whites could have afforded. Everyone was braced for them to have it out again. To tell the truth my money was on Nickell. I had Miller down as a man with a yellow streak. it ain't right to pull a knife in a fist fight. But the next thing we knew, Kell's little boy, Willie, was shot in the back as he was opening their gate one morning, about three quarters of a mile from the house. The murderous son of a bitch who shot him did so from the cover of an outcrop up the slope a good ways, then lit out like the dirty dog he was. The Millers was forted up and sobbing that they'd just loved that boy and hadn't even gone outside to feed the chickens that morning. There was no way to blame one with the others all swearing alibis. Kell Nickell didn't swear at all. We've been waiting ever since to see who makes the next move. If I was you, I wouldn't go anywheres near the scene of the tragedy."

"I thank you for your words of warning," Stringer said dryly. "Would it be too much to ask if you had any notion why Tom Horn was the one the law finally decided on?"

"Well, I'm just a cowhand, not a politician. But if I *was* a politician, I might have noticed that Tom Horn ain't registered to vote in this county and that both the Nickell and Miller clans got a lot of friends and relations who are," Casey opined.

Stringer nodded grimly. "I follow your drift. Horn was not only an outsider but a sort of mysterious stranger who no doubt made a lot of locals nervous as well."

Casey grinned. "I'd hate to be a cattle thief with old Tom Horn running loose. And he was an awful pain in the ass to everyone when he was drunk."

Stringer didn't answer. "Why don't you just let her go at that, Mister MacKail?" Casey asked. "The death of that boy seems to have shocked the Nickells and Millers to their senses and Tom Horn is no great loss to anyone, right?"

"Wrong," Stringer said. "If he's innocent he has as much right to live as any other useless son of a bitch, damnit."

Stringer found the smithy closed and shuttered. There'd have been no sense leaving his gear in the smith's tack room if he hadn't expected them to lock the damned door. But it was really starting to get nippy now. Stringer banged on the front door for a spell and when that didn't work he headed around to the side.

He met the gal called Cherokee coming around the corner the other way, with a wool shawl around her bare shoulders. "I was coming to fetch you," she said. "I told you that you'd find it noisy in that saloon."

He said, "You did and I owe you, ma'am. How come you're taking such an interest?"

Cherokee laughed bitterly. "Maybe you remind me of the son I never had. Maybe I just don't like noise. Come on. My place is just across the tracks. The town's too small to say if I live on the right side of the tracks or the wrong. Suffice it to say I have no close or nosy neighbors."

He hesitated. Then he shrugged and said, "Anything has to beat sleeping on the dew-wet grass without a blanket. But how much is all this hospitality apt to cost me, ma'am?"

She swore under her breath and told him, "I'm not a landlady, either. If you must know, I have my own good reasons for keeping the gunplay in these parts down to a roar. If that gunslick who was looking for you has any friends within miles..."

"Lead on." He cut in, adding, "I hate to wake up with straw in my hair when it might be safer somewhere else."

They circled the smithy and corrals out back and crossed a single line of railroad track. Stringer had ridden across the same coming in and had found it curious the first time. So he asked her, "Would you know where this spur line runs to, ma'am?"

"Sure," she said. "Cheyenne, going south. I think the other way takes you to the North Platte. Why?"

"I never noticed any such tracks, riding all that way this afternoon."

"That's because the wagon trace beelines straight across the rises between here and the county seat. I guess railroads have to run along one level. That takes some doing in such bumpy country. Is there any point to all this railroad talk?"

"Well, I would have needed that roan once I got here, anyway. It just shoots a couple of suspicions I was chewing on all to hell. I reckon old Winfield Scott Rutherford got up here the smart way. That would account for his not having a mount tied up anywheres around here."

She pointed to a dark mass looming in the moonlight ahead of them and said, "That's my cabin. Was that the gunslick's name?"

"We're still working on that," he replied. "The point is that he could have heard which way I was headed, from a lot of folk, long after I left Cheyenne, and still beat me here by an hour if he came up by train."

They got to her door. He noticed she paused to unlock it even though there couldn't be more than a few dozen folk living in the whole settlement when the herds were not in town. She wasn't wired for Edison bulbs out here in the middle of nowhere, of course. So the table lamp she lit cast a moody light. He was too polite to say her lamp chimney needed cleaning. She adjusted the wick knob to burn a mite brighter, then said, "That's better. Let's see if I get this straight. You suspected someone down at the county seat of telling that other idiot where you were going?"

"Somebody had to, and it wasn't me. But as I look back on it, I told all sorts of folk I meant to ride up this way for a look-see, by the time I'd hired a mount and all. I liked it better when I had it down to just two or three. Now I'm back where I started with a whole world of mysterious strangers to worry about."

She told him to sit himself down and went someplace mysterious for a spell. He chose the leather chesterfield against one plank wall. It wasn't as comfortable as it looked until he found a spot where the horsehair padding was still in place over the springs. The rest of her front room was furnished with the same slapdash care. Nothing looked new and nothing matched. The place smelled clean and he could see she dusted now and again. So she was either poor, didn't give a hang, or she'd moved into a small town suddenly with no great desire to stay for good. Her fancy duds were professionally fitted to her curves, as he recalled, and it cost money to get one's hair dyed, even though right now old Cherokee could use a touch-up. She'd likely found both her seamstress and that beauty shop in a somewhat more advanced part of the world.

She came back into her parlor bearing a japanned tin tray of coffee and cake. She placed it before the chesterfield on a soap box she'd converted to a coffee table and sat down beside him. The cake was marble, store-bought, and a mite stale. But she made good coffee and he was hungry enough to eat anything, once he dunked it soft enough to bite into.

Stringer was country raised and hence inclined to eat and get it over with. But since working his way through Stanford and seeing more of the world, he'd learned less rustic folk liked to jaw about life as they chewed. Whatever Cherokee might be, rustic was not the word for her. So he thought it only polite to bring her up to date on who he was and why he was in Iron Mountain.

She poured them both more coffee as she said, "I arrived well after that Nickell boy was murdered so I wouldn't know Tom Horn or Joe LeFors if I woke up in bed with them." She smiled wryly. "That sounds like fun, or disgusting, depending on what they look like."

He grinned and said, "I can't speak for Joe LeFors. But old Tom could be mistaken for a distinguished middle-aged man if he didn't look sort of stupid as well."

"I like 'em young and athletic," she said, smiling big at Stringer. "But let's stick to the less romantic trouble you've been messing with. Like I said, I wasn't here when that boy was bushwhacked, but I've been here long enough to know the smell of the aftermath. You're asking for trouble with at least three factions, uh . . . Stringer?"

"Stringer's close enough. Who might you want to name as the rascal who keeps trying to scare me off the case?"

"I hardly think that last try for you in the saloon tonight was meant as just a threat. As to the who of it, I'll give you your choice between the C.P.A., the Millers, or the Nickells."

Stringer sipped some coffee as he considered her cheering words. Then he said, "Maybe. I can see why the cattle barons who hired Tom Horn might want to let that sleeping dog hang, whether he did it or not. They can't afford the publicity since the range wars of the nineties almost persuaded Washington to close all the open range, and of course, if Tom's got any back pay coming for services rendered . . . Nope, they'd hardly pay hired guns to stop me from helping Tom get free enough to bill 'em."

He drained the cup, then shook his head when she started to pour him another, saying, "No, thanks, ma'am. Not if I aim to sleep at all tonight. I can see why the Miller faction might be upset by my snooping about, if they really murdered Willie Nickell the way a lot of folk suspect. But why in thunder would the Nickell clan be worried about an investigative reporter looking into the death of one of their own?"

"That's easy," she said. "Tom Horn's been convicted of the crime."

He scowled at her and demanded, "Why would they want the law to hang the wrong man for spilling the blood of a kinsman? I mean, sure, they likely think Tom Horn did it. So they'd likely want to hang him themselves, with trimmings. But the only way anyone is about to get Tom Horn off is by exposing some other cuss as the real killer.

If I was Kell Nickell I'd be pleased as punch to see the man who really killed my boy arrested."

She stared at him curiously and said, "MacKail's a Scotch name, isn't it?"

He asked just what that had to do with Wyoming feuds.

"I've read about the way your Scotch clans carried on over spilt blood," she said. "It's no wonder the English wound up running the place. You fighting fools didn't know how to *end* a feud. Neither the Nickells nor the Millers came west to spend the next hundred years or so taking pot shots at one another. It's hard enough to make a living raising stock on this poor range."

Stringer said, "I was told how the feud flared up with a sudden fight that turned ugly. I agree it makes sense to end such a profitless feud. But surely if I was to manage to expose the real killer of Willie Nickell . . ."

"The Nickells would have to go after the Millers as a point of family honor," she cut in. "The Millers, in turn, would feel honor-bound to deny the charge and defend their accused kinsman to the death. Both factions could field a lot of friends and relations. So it would mean an all-out war, and naturally, once the state guard was called in, both sides would likely be crushed and driven out of Wyoming."

He pursed his lips and decided, "That's how the Lincoln County War down New Mexico Way wound up, all right. But I don't recall the Murphy Faction covering up for Billy the Kid after he took to gunning 'em some."

She said, "Maybe Murphy didn't mind starting over in other parts after neither he nor the Kid's side wound up owning anything after all that gunplay. Both the Nickells and the Millers got land and herds to hang on to. They no doubt hate one another as much or more than ever. But with both sides sobered by Mister Death's sour breath, and a man with no kin on either side about to pay Mister Death's grim bill..."

"That works, and it's mean-spirited as hell," he cut in. Then he asked, "Do you think Joseph Miller killed Willie Nickell, too?"

Cherokee shrugged her bare shoulders. "I wasn't there. So I'm not saying. But he had the motive and a bad enough temper to knife a man in a fistfight. I understand a lot of people accused him of the deed at the time. But since then they've learned not to. Like I said, a nasty temper and the friends to back his play. You might say Deputy Marshal LeFors performed an important public service by arresting Tom Horn for the deed. That way both sides can say they're satisfied and nobody has to get hurt."

He growled, "Nobody but Tom Horn, you mean," and she sighed.

"There's an outside possibility he's guilty," she replied, "but it's not as if we're talking about Bo Peep, you know. That old hired gun has surely gotten away with many a murder in his time and if Willie Nickell wasn't one of 'em, tough. Are you ready to turn in, yet? I know I am."

He repressed a yawn and said, "I did promise to meet the town law early in the morning. But let me help you with them cups and saucers first, Miss Cherokee."

"You just make yourself at home whilst I put these things in the dry sink," she said rising. "I got an Indian woman who comes around noon to tidy up for me."

He didn't argue. As she headed to the kitchen he took off his gun rig, wadded his hat and jacket up like a sort of pillow, and experimented with stretching out on the battered chesterfield. The experiment didn't work. Stringer was well over six feet long, even if he took his boots off, and the chesterfield stretched less than five feet between its padded arms. It was hard and lumpy, no matter where he tried to put his hip.

But he figured it still had the floor or the night prairie beat. He wondered if he was supposed to trim the lamp or if his hostess meant to come back and do it. It was dark on the far side of the archway leading back to the rest of the cabin and she was as likely to cuss him as to thank him if he left her floundering about in total darkness.

He saw he'd chosen correctly when she did come back in, shot him a startled look, then asked, "Are you really comfortable on that sofa?"

"No. But I've bunked worse places and it was kind of you to offer, ma'am."

"Suit yourself," she shrugged, and flounced out. He tried to roll over. His knees wouldn't fit that way either. He told himself to just lay still and that he'd fall asleep, comfortable or not, if he was really tired. He closed his eyes. He could see the lamp light through his lids. He wondered why she hadn't trimmed it or taken it with her. Women never seemed to do things the way a man expected them to. They weren't exactly dumb or crazy. They just didn't seem to see things the way men did. That was no doubt why they were always moving furniture around to no good purpose any man could fathom.

He couldn't get comfortable. He was sorry now he'd had that strong coffee. Then he heard her softly speak his name and opened his eyes, now feeling wide awake. She was standing in the archway without a thing on, unless you wanted to count a black velvet garter as duds. As he stared up at her voluptuous nude form, trying to formulate something sensible to say, she asked softly, "Would you really rather spend the night on that lumpy sofa?"

So in no time at all they were in her big brass bedstead and she was saying adoringly, "I knew you were too long for that sofa, but I never dared hope you'd be *this* long. Let me slide this pillow out from under my hips. We don't seem to need it after all, and I'm so glad, aren't you?"

He didn't answer. He was coming and he liked that pillow where it was, just fine. She gasped in mingled passion and dismay as he went on hitting bottom with every stroke. Then she wedged her soft thighs up to hug his heaving ribs with a shapely knee tucked in both his armpits as she crooned, "Oh, that's better. That's heavenly, darling. Aren't you going to say your sorry for mistaking me for a whore?"

He kissed her soft throat, ejaculated in her hard, and kept moving politely as he growled, "I don't know what you are, but you do this too fine for a lady not to have her heart set on it."

She moaned passionately, dug her nails into his buttocks, and climaxed with protracted pulsations, inspiring him to greater effort. Then she went stiff and cold in his arms, demanding hoarsely, "Just what did you mean by that?"

He stopped moving in her to stare down at her suddenly hard face. "Hell's bells, what did you think I meant by all this motion, girl?" he asked. "I thought you were enjoying it as much as I was."

"I'm not talking about *that,*" she snarled. *"That* feels just lovely. What was that remark about my not being what I say I am?"

He kissed her. Her lips were primmed like a pissed-off virgin's. "Hell, Cherokee, I was just making conversation. Would you rather I called you a whore instead?"

"I want to know what you think I really am, damn you and your steel-trap eye for details and nose for news."

He rolled off and fumbled for the shirt he'd draped over

one brass bedpost as he told her, "If you ask me, you're the one who snaps suspicious around here. You told me before that you're a lady cardshark. The reason I suspected you of whoring is that I'll be whipped with snakes if I can see how even a gal as pretty as you could make a dishonest living in a settlement this size, dealing dirty and screwing dirty combined."

She sat up on one elbow and stared down hard at him. "All right. So I'm not in Cheyenne where all the action is right now. Are you saying I'm hiding out in this trail town, Stringer?"

He began to roll a smoke as he said, "I liked it better when you were calling me darling. If I confess such thoughts might have crossed my mind, will you stop shooting daggers at me with those big dark eyes?"

She wouldn't. "You bastard! All that guff about Tom Horn was just a cover-up. And to think I was so worried about you and... My God, I'm smack in bed with you! Are you going to arrest me yourself, or just turn me in to Jim Tate in the morning, you brute?"

Stringer sealed the Bull Durham with his tongue before he muttered, "Maybe someday I'll have women figured out. I hope I won't be so old by that time that it won't matter. You're not making a lick of sense, Cherokee."

"Oh, no? Next thing you'll tell me you never even guessed I could be..."

"Stop." He cut in, firmly, and when she did he said, "I don't want to guess who you might really be. I'm a newspaperman, not the law, and I've already got enough on my plate for a man who only came to cover those Frontier Days. In case you forgot what happened earlier this evening, I did come up here to ask about the murder of Willie Nickell and I'd no sooner started asking when someone tried to murder me. So unless that gent in the red shirt was a pal of yours—and you were acting mighty odd if he was—you saved my life by warning me in time about the way he wore his gun, and I said I owed you. So even if you didn't make good coffee and screw like a mink I'd feel mighty dirty turning you in, even if I knew what they wanted you for. Since I don't, I won't. You have my word on that. Where in hell did I put my fool matches?"

As he groped for his jacket on the floor with the smoke unlit between his own tight lips, Cherokee's lips softened. "I'm sorry," she said. "You're likely telling it true, as soon as a girl studies on it. It's just that I'm so tired of being on the dodge and..."

"Shut up," he said flatly. Then he found a match and stuck a light. As he did so he could see her big warm eyes were filled with tears. He lit his smoke, shook out the match, and growled, "Aw, don't blubber up on me. I didn't mean to speak so sharp, honey. I only said shut up because I don't want you saying dumb things you might regret in the cold gray light of dawn."

As they snuggled back down together, sharing the smoke, the mystery woman of Iron Mountain sighed and said, "You're right. The last person I should tell my tale to would be a newspaperman." Then she repressed a giggle and added, "So far, the newspapers have gotten so much about us all wrong."

He didn't answer. Her body felt soft and warm against his. But he was starting to feel a distinct chill. For try as he might not to study on who Cherokee might or might not be, she was starting to fit. Despite Ned Buntline, very few outlaw gals of the West had ever been really good-looking. So that, and the real color of her hair, narrowed it down considerable. He hoped he was wrong. But just the same, when she wanted to get on top he let her.

CHAPTER SIX

After Cherokee served him a cold breakfast and some more warm loving in the morning light Stringer met old Jim Tate, the town law, at the saloon as they'd agreed. Tate said, "I've been on the telly-phone to Cheyenne already. It's hard to get anyone to talk to you with everyone excited about that wild west show down yonder. If it was up to me, they'd hold her all one day and get it over with."

"Maybe someday they will," Stringer said. "Right now, between the stock judging, cake raffles, and Lord knows what all, they just don't have time to do her all at once, like you say. Did you find out anything at all?"

"Yeah. I found out the copper badge who's supposed to keep track of the infernal files has agreed to judge a damn calf riding contest for kids. Why in the hell would they ask a law officer to act as a damned old rodeo judge?"

"To keep folk from saying the judging might not have been honest, I reckon. Since the contestants themselves have to chip in the prize money to be awarded the winner, the losers tend to bitch a lot when they lose by a point or so. It's best to have such points awarded by a gent with a rep for honesty. Did you think to call anyone on the entrance committee, Jim? They'd surely know if they had any kind of a Winfield Scott listed as a contestant."

The older man looked disgusted. "They don't. That was easy to check off. He must have just liked loud shirts naturally. It's the police record of the cuss interests me, but with not a soul willing to go through the damned old yellow sheets for me I'm pure stuck for now."

"You could always try Hayes," Stringer suggested. "That's where his voter's card said he was from."

Old Jim frowned. "Hayes, *Kansas,* by telly-phone?"

So Stringer had to explain how one got Central to hook one up for a long-distance telephone call and added that the county could be billed for it.

Jim Tate whistled. "Well, I never. I ain't never called nobody *that* far off on the telly-phone, son. You'd best come along and show me how. They got the contraption set up in the general store next door."

Stringer nodded and followed the older man into the attached retail establishment. A pretty young gal was tending shop. Old Jim introduced her as the daughter of old Fats. Stringer didn't argue. Anything was possible and Fats was more fat than ugly.

The deputy told her they wanted to use the telly-phone some more and she led them down to the far end of her counter, where a wall-mounted telephone was half hidden by some bales. Jim Tate told Stringer to go first. So the younger conspirator took the earpiece off its hook, cranked a spell, and once he got the reedy voice of Central, shouted out they wanted the sheriff's department in Hayes, Kansas. Central seemed just as astounded by the idea as Tate had been, but after Stringer explained how it might be done, twice, she consulted someone else and told him, "You'll have to try again in about half an hour. My supervisor's not here and I just don't know how to connect anyone to *Kansas!*"

Stringer hung up, turned to the old deputy, and said, "Give her until, say, seven-thirty and it might work. If I know it can be done, the odds are that a supervisor might."

As he started to leave, Jim Tate protested, "Hold on, where will you be if I need you, damnit?"

"You won't need me," Stringer said. "Either way. If they can do it at all they'll know how to get you through. I thought I'd ride out to where that kid got bushwhacked, if it's all the same to you, Jim."

"Like hell it is! I don't want you poking about out yonder, Stringer. I already have one shoot-out here in Iron Mountain to write up."

Stringer smiled thinly. "Are you offering an opinion that the killer of Willie Nickell might still be at large, Jim?"

The old man looked flustered and said, "Don't you go putting dumb words in my mouth, damnit. It ain't for me to say who might or might not have shot that kid. I wasn't the arresting officer."

"I know. I wondered more about that before I got here than I've learned to since." Then he turned away and strode out. Old Jim didn't try to stop him.

The blacksmith was willing to give Stringer the simple directions to the place where Willie Nickell died. It would have been overtly rude not to. But as he helped Stringer saddle up he added, "I wouldn't go over there this morning if I was you. It looks like rain."

"I've got a spur-length slicker in this roll and you just said it was a short ride," Stringer said.

The smith tried again. "You won't find either Kell

Nickell nor old man Miller at home. They both went down to Cheyenne for the stock showings this week."

Stringer shrugged. "I'll just have a look around." He led the roan outside to mount up. But as he swung himself into the saddle the smith said flatly, "Don't go. You're just asking for trouble, son."

Stringer glanced up at the sky. It was only a mite overcast and the wind was still from the west. He said, "I'll likely be there and back before it clouds up enough to matter." Then he spurred his mount forward as the smith bawled something after him that was lost in the clatter of hoofbeats on gravel.

Stringer only had to watch for a couple of forks in the well-beaten trails that were running mostly upslope from the bitty town. He counted the fence lines marking the boundaries of the modest-sized homestead claims on the way to Iron Mountain. As he spied a stone outcrop on a rise ahead he slowed his mount to a walk. "That sure answers to the description of the cover the killer fired from. Let's see if we can find us a break in that bob wire ahead," he muttered to the horse.

That was easy. The beaten path they were following took them to an improvised gate of the same wire strung on an aspen-pole frame. Stringer dismounted and tethered his mount to a post. As he did so he noticed an oval of good-sized rocks laid out in the grass just off the beaten path. Each rock was about the size and weight a man could handle with two hands and not much sweat. They enclosed an area just about right for a short man or half-grown boy to stretch out on the grass. Stringer hunkered down just outside the oval as he tried to picture just how Willie Nickell's young body might have fit inside the improvised monument.

He glanced upslope at the outcrop and muttered to himself, "Whether he landed face down or face up, his head would have been farthest from the killer's rifle blast up yonder. They put these rocks all around his body to mark this spot for the law before they carried him home."

He combed the grass stubble inside and around the rocks for a sign but wasn't surprised to find none. A couple of winters had swept by the spartan monument since Willie Nickell had gasped his last breath here, and naturally a whole mess of lawmen had already combed the grass dry for yards around.

Stringer rose, climbed through the wire without opening it, and legged it up to that rock outcrop everyone said the killer had fired from. Stringer didn't expect to find any spent shells or remains of the raw bacon Tom Horn liked to chew on such tedious occasions. He moved around to hunker behind the outcrop just as the killer would have, and thanks to the clearly visible oval of rocks down below, he was able to decide, half aloud, "Yep, an easy rifle shot from here. But anyone sober enough to hit his target from here would have had a hell of a time mistaking a skinny kid for his full-grown father."

Stringer got up again and moved slowly and thoughtfully down the slope, along the track the fatal bullet would have taken. If the boy had been given the morning chore of opening that gate for his sheep to move out to open range, it would have been broad-ass daylight in fair weather. Even with the overcast this particular morning Stringer could make out individual details, and Tom Horn didn't wear specs.

It was still possible he'd done it drunk, of course. But while two hundred yards was an easy rifle shot for a man who knew what he was doing, it was a mite far for shooting wild.

As he approached the fence line again Stringer noticed a

half-dozen riders approaching from the other direction. They'd been moving at a lope. As they spotted him they reined their ponies to a walk but kept coming. By the time Stringer made it back to his own tethered mount they were lined up, sort of looming at him. He recognized one as Sweet Violets Vance. So he said howdy.

Sweet Violets didn't answer. An older and harder-looking rider growled, "You had no call to mess with them rocks, Pilgrim. Them rocks was put there by orders of James Miller hisself."

Stringer said, "Now that's sort of interesting. Which rock was under the dead boy's head?"

The obvious leader scowled and said, "You sure talk wise-ass for a stranger nobody never invited to poke about out here."

"I thought Sweet Violets there was an old pal of mine," Stringer smiled. "Who might you be, friend?"

The spokesman for the roughly dressed group said, "You don't want to know who we are, MacKail. For if we thought you was about to appear in court against us we'd have to make sure you never."

Stringer asked mildly, "Why would I have call to take you boys to law?"

Another rider laughed and said, "Because we mean to teach you some manners and there's an outside chance you'll live through it."

The one who seemed to be the leader nodded and began to shake out his throw rope. "You never should have messed with them rocks," he said. "Now we'll have to drag you some to pay you back."

Stringer said, "Hold the thought. You boys ain't as incognito as you might think. I know Sweet Violets there, and he'll surely lead me and mine to the rest of you later, if I ask him nicely."

There was a moment of confusion. Then the leader replied, "That's likely true. We'd best make sure you don't wind up in condition to pester any of us—ever." Then he threw.

Stringer had been expecting him to. He sidestepped the spinning loop, caught it with both hands, and ran with it until he was in position to jerk it hard from the roper's awkward side. It almost spilled horse and rider. But not quite. And by now two others were trying to rope Stringer. He hopscotched clear and dove headfirst through the barbwire fence. He landed on his left shoulder and came up, hatless, with his gun in his right hand. He fired it once in the air and snapped, "That's enough, boys."

The leader began to snake and regather his rope as he laughed and said, "Not hardly. I was sort of hoping you'd draw a weapon on me, Pilgrim. For now, as anyone here can see, we are dealing with a homicidal lunatic and a man has a right to protect himself, right?"

Sweet Violets said, "Hold on, Spud. Nobody said nothing about gunplay and the man has at least four left in his wheel."

The one called Spud finished recoiling his rope and snorted, "So what? There's six of us, ain't there?"

Sweet Violets shook his head. "Five. You can count me out. I've seen him shoot." Then he whistled his pony and rode off fast, not looking back.

"Always figured a man who wore chaps when there was no need to had to be a four-flusher," Spud said, turning to Stringer. "You'd best drop that gun, MacKail. We might let you live if you're willing to take a little dragging like a good sport. But like Sweet Violets just said, you don't have enough bullets to take on the five of us, and the one left is sure to finish you off slow and dirty."

Stringer shrugged and said, "That sounds reasonable. Now I want all five of you to dismount, hands polite."

Spud looked more surprised than upset as he asked, "Ain't you been paying attention? There's no way in hell you can hope to down the five of us with four rounds. So drop that damn gun afore someone gets hurt."

"Get down from that horse," Stringer demanded. "You have my promise true that I'll kill you first, if it takes all four of my rounds."

Spud gulped, "Aw, hell, let's let him go, boys."

It didn't work. Stringer said, "The first one of you who puts spur to flank figures to be first one down. I told you all to dismount. I'm not going to say it again."

So the five of them dismounted. Then Stringer said, "That's better. Now I want to see some gun rigs in the grass. Unbuckle 'em and let 'em drop, unless you want to drop with 'em."

Spud protested, "Are you going to let one sissy newspaperman get away with this, boys?"

"Yep," an older and wiser-looking rider replied. "He's got the drop on us and Sweet Violets told us from starting that he was damn handy with that gun."

There was a sheepish murmur of agreement and soon everyone but Spud had let his weaponry fall from easy reach. Spud swore, "Well, hell, if nobody around here has the hair on his chest to back a pard, I can't see slapping leather on a man who has me covered cold."

Stringer waited until Spud had let his gun fall at his feet before he nodded and said, "That's better. Now your pants."

"My *what?*"

"I want you to unbutton those jeans and take 'em off," Stringer explained nicely.

"What are you, some kind of a queer?" Spud protested.

Stringer just laughed lightly and replied, "What's the matter? Can't you take a joke? I thought you boys rode out here looking for some fun. Show us how funny you are, Spud. Or would you rather die more dignified? I'll count to ten. Then I'll kill you if you've still got those pants on."

He sounded like he meant it. Even some of his pals were laughing by the time the red-faced Spud had shucked his jeans to expose his skinny legs. Stringer was trying to make up his mind about the rest of them when they all heard a distant hail and saw four more riders coming in.

Stringer was beginning to worry about just how many gents one man can rawhide with only four bullets as the newcomers reined in. One called out, "Deputy Tate sent us to fetch you, Stringer. What's going on here?"

Stringer called back, "Me and the boys were just having a little fun. What's up?"

The lawman who seemed to be in command laughed and replied, "It sure ain't old Spud's pants. What's wrong with him? Has he got ticks?"

Spud bawled, "This stranger throwed down on us and, as you see, forced me to pants myself at gunpoint. I want the rascal arrested for indecent exposure, Whitey!"

The lawman laughed and answered, "You seem to be the one who's waving his fool pecker in the breeze, Spud. Pull your damn pants up and behave yourself. Was they giving you a hard time, MacKail?"

Stringer reloaded as he shook his head and said, "I don't think Spud could show it hard for Queen Cleopatra at the moment. Like I said, they were just out to green a dude and I feel sure they've seen the error of their ways. I'm willing to say it's over if they are."

Whitey nodded at Spud, who was blushing like a rose as he buttoned his jeans back on, and asked, "How about that, Spud? Is it over?"

Spud said, "Aw, hell, I ain't about to go after nobody if my own friends won't show me a little backing and respect." So the leader of the second party nodded at Stringer and said, "It's over. We'd best get you back to town, Stringer. Deputy Tate said he was in a hurry to see you. He takes things more serious than these assholes you've been playing games with."

Stringer found old Deputy Jim seated at the saloon table Cherokee usually had spread with cards. Neither she nor any of the other regulars were there that early in the day. Stringer sat down across from the old lawman and asked what he should be worrying about now.

"I finally got through to Hayes," Tate replied. "They still have some bugs to work out of that Bell System. Hayes says the real Winfield Scott Rutherford is dead. Shot in a card game by a trash white called Billy Gower, about six weeks ago."

Stringer shrugged. "Well, it was worth a try. That gent in the red silk shirt might not have wanted to use his real name for some reason."

"He was Billy Gower," Tate explained. "Hayes recalled that same shirt, that tie-down holster, and the other ways I described the man you shot to 'em."

"He must have kept and cherished the I.D. as well as the wallet he got off the real Rutherford," Stringer suggested.

"That's the way me and Hayes sees it," Tate said. "Gower had good reason to carry false I.D. Under his right handle, he was wanted for everything but spreading typhoid, and he might have done that if he'd knowed how. He was a vicious son of a bitch. Too trigger-happy to ride with a regular gang. He went in for lonesome robbing and killing. I don't think he was out to rob you last night. Since he was asking for you by name before he found out how unwise that could be, I'd say someone sent him after you. His record includes hired assassination as a sort of sideline."

Stringer got out the makings and began to roll a smoke. "The possibility had already crossed my mind. Do you think the C.P.A. would hire such a wild man, Jim?" he asked.

"Not hardly," Tate replied. "Even Tom Horn had a range detective's license afore he got too wild and they had to throw him to the wolves. What if he was a pal of Horn, hisself? Old Tom would drink with anybody and..."

"I can't see Tom Horn sending anyone to gun me," Stringer cut in, explaining, "I never would have shown any interest in his sort of stale story if he hadn't sent for me himself, and asked me to go over it all again. It seems a lot more likely someone else wants to let sleeping dogs lie so Horn can hang. I'll be damned if I can figure out what they're worried about, though. I was just out to the murder scene, and to tell the truth I didn't see a thing that could prove Tom Horn did or didn't do it."

He lit his smoke and asked, "What happens next about the late Billy Gower? Has your local coroner come back yet?"

The old deputy looked uncomfortable as he said, "No. Doc Marvin ain't due back for a few days. That's one of the things I wanted to talk to you about."

"Jesus, I can't hang around here that long!" Stringer swore.

Tate said, "Don't get your bowels in an uproar. That's what I wanted to talk to you about."

He hesitated, then continued, "Like I said, the late Billy Gower was wanted lots of places and he had...uh...

considerable bounty money posted on his otherwise useless hide."

The penny dropped. Stringer grinned. "That's mighty interesting, Jim. Ain't it a good thing the *law* got him when he made the mistake of passing through Iron Mountain?"

The old and no doubt underpaid deputy grinned like a mean little kid. "I was sort of hoping we could come to a meeting of the minds on that bounty money," he said. "I've been setting here trying to figure just how I should word my claim. You're the writer. Suppose you tell me?"

"It's always best to keep things short and simple, Jim," Stringer said. "If you were to simply say Billy Gower was spotted in your jurisdiction acting suspicious, and that he wound up dead as you were fixing to question him, and that you'd sure like that money posted on him, now..."

"Ain't that sort of fibbing?" the old deputy cut in.

"Well, it's sure a sin to write a lie," the younger man said. "I'm not sure it's wrong to leave out pesky details. It's the usual custom for the man who downs a dead-or-alive to put himself in for the reward. And since everyone ought to be delighted to hear the rascal's dead..."

Old Jim said, "Say no more. That's about the way I'd read it if I got such a terse cheerful message. I reckon I know how to word it. But are you sure you don't want a cut, son?"

Stringer looked innocent and asked, "How could I claim part of the bounty, Jim? I'm not connected to your department and it was your department brought that rascal to justice at last, wasn't it?"

"I wish you could stick around longer, Stringer. I'm really getting mighty fond of you," old Jim chuckled.

"Then I'm free to leave?"

"I got no call to keep you here. The law don't need no

witness when a knowed killer gets shot down pure and simple. But I hope you don't mean to ride for Cheyenne right now."

"Sure I do. I did what I came up here to do and a little more. I was hoping to stumble over something that might help poor Tom Horn. But I never did, and meanwhile, I can still cover at least the closing ceremonies of that rodeo."

Tate said, "Lord willing and the creeks don't rise. They're sure fixing to. It's fixing to rain fire and salt outside."

"I sure hope so. If it starts raining this side of high noon they'll have to cancel today's contests down at the Cheyenne fair grounds. I've got a sidekick trying to fill in for me. But to tell the truth he's not as cow as me," Stringer laughed, "and I'd rather do it myself."

As he rose from the table the old deputy insisted, "You're more likely to wind up drowned if you ride out afore the wind makes up her mind, Stringer. That's a good day's ride, dry, and I'll bet you ten bucks we're in for a real gully-washer afore sundown."

Stringer said, "No bet. I noticed the sky earlier. It's more like a five-hour ride aboard a good mount, and it'll be cooler riding if it rains."

The old deputy followed him to the door, insisting he'd never make it across some prairie draws he knew of without a ferry boat. But Stringer knew he was secretly glad. So they shook and parted friendly. Then Stringer got the same argument when he picked his mount up again at the smithy.

As Stringer broke out his big yellow slicker and strapped it where a throw rope might have gone if he'd had one the smith said, "I'd wait them rain clouds out if I was you. They're boiling so that we could just get a sudden, if not mighty awesome summer storm. Can't you find some place to sort of bed down until that sky makes up her mind?"

"I might," Stringer said, "but a smart man quits while he's ahead."

He saw no need to explain as he forked himself aboard the roan and rode off. But he knew a man could get in more trouble indoors than out, messing with the wrong woman, and if Cherokee was who she'd begun to add up to, he could only hope she'd never tell anyone about the way she'd yielded to her natural lonesome longings the night before.

The roan was nervous about the way the sky was growling down at them as they headed south. Stringer took advantage of this by running him down the long slopes of the rolling prairie, and a horse could still walk upslope faster than any man could. They couldn't see the sun. But well before it could have been directly overhead, a big wet thunderbird turd splashed down on Stringer's hat brim. He reached for his slicker with a sigh, muttering, "Someone sure means to water the grass good today."

His shoulders were already wet by the time he had the stiff linseed-scented slicker on. He'd chosen it with such events in mind. It covered his bedroll and some of the roan's rump as well as his own, right down to the stirrups. The rest of his mount got to shiver in the pelting rain. "You'll feel warmer if you move faster," he told the animal, spurring it to a steady lope. The grass all around turned wet welcome-mat brown and the dark sky kept getting darker when lighting wasn't flashing and spooking the roan.

They made good time for close to an hour. But Stringer knew he had to rest his mount at least a few minutes out of every hour and he reined in when they came to a low draw, out of the worst of the wind. But as they tried to rest down there, in fetlock-deep running water with a lot more of the same coming straight down, lightning struck atop a rise too close for comfort and Stringer almost got to ride back to Iron Mountain unplanned.

He patted the roan's wet neck with a dripping palm and told it, "You're right. There has to be a better way. Unless we're lost entire, I recall a soddy we passed coming up this way. It was mayhaps half a mile off the wagon trace, to the east. Let's see if it's still there."

The roan didn't argue. They still had a time finding shelter with the storm waving silvery veils between them and anything at all distant. But just as Stringer was sure they were headed the wrong way he spied the low dark mass of the homestead he'd noticed before on a brighter occasion. As they rode in he noticed great minds seemed to run in the same channels. A line of ponies were tethered under the overhang of a pole and sod-roofed open shed. Stringer put his own mount in with the others and sloshed his way across the ankle-deep dooryard to the main house. As he got there the door opened and an old gent in bib overalls said, "I thought I heard more hoof-beats out here in this deluge. Come on in, son. My old woman ain't had this much fun since the Seventh Cav dropped by in Seventy-seven."

Stringer followed the old nester inside, peeling off his slicker to keep from dripping all over the dirt floor. Five other soggy-looking riders were seated around a plank table in the crowded soddy. A sweet old motherly woman by the cook-stove told Stringer to set himself right down. So he did. The interior of her thick-walled little house smelled like coffee, mud, apple pie, and horse shit, all mixed together warm and homey.

Stringer introduced himself. The burly gent sitting next

to him said he was Deputy U.S. Marshal Jacobs and that the other four had been riding with him until they almost wound up at the bottom of the sea outside.

Stringer asked if they were working under the well-known Joe LeFors.

Jacobs growled, "That'll be the day. Last I heard of LeFors he was over in the Hole In The Wall Country with his fancy railroad car. A lot he knows about catching the Wild Bunch."

Another federal rider said, "There ain't no such thing as no hole in no wall. Butch and Sundance only hide out in rough country nobody else is using between jobs. They'd be crazy if they was camped anywhere near their usual haunts with LeFors and all them others chasing 'em aboard a special train."

The sweet old woman at the stove commenced pouring coffee and her husband began to spread the tin cups on the table for their rain-chilled guests. Deputy Jacobs said, "Lord bless you and keep you folk. You're still gonna have to let us pay you afore we ride out for Iron Mountain, though."

The old nester told them not to talk dirty in front of his wife. "I just rode down from Iron Mountain. What are you boys interested in, that shoot-out last night?" Stringer asked.

Jacobs frowned at him and asked what he was talking about. "They got an owlhoot called Billy Gower last night," Stringer said. "Had a mess of rewards posted on him, I hear."

Jacobs grimaced and said, "I've heard of that puddle of scum. I'm pleased to hear they got him. But he was never wanted on any federal charges. We're after bigger fish."

One of his sidekicks chimed in, "Etta Place, the Sundance Kid's play-pretty."

Stringer sipped some coffee. It felt better than it tasted going down. Then he said, "Last I heard of Sundance, he'd been seen back East. They say he hailed from New Jersey to begin with. Didn't he make the mistake of having his fool self photographed in a New York studio, along with that school marm he ran off with?"

Jacobs said, "I doubts even Joe LeFors bought that ruse. I can't say whether Etta Place started out as a schoolmarm or a cow town... uh... remember the ladies present, gents."

He sipped at his own tin cup before he went on explaining. "A lot of old boys thought it was sort of dumb for Butch and Sundance to pose for studio photographs, considering how well known they've recently become. The New York P.D. even scouted up the ticket agency where they bought steamship tickets for South America, and if there's one thing Mister Robert Leroy Parker alias Butch Cassidy ain't, it's dumb enough to do a dumb thing like that."

Another deputy explained, "They bought them steamship tickets under their right names, Parker and Longabaugh, not Butch and Sundance."

Stringer opined, "Well, either way, they were long gone for South America by the time anyone noticed, right?"

Jacobs shook his head. "You mean if they ever left the country at all," he said. "The one thing Joe LeFors and me agree upon is that neither of them rascals speak Spanish and that trains are still being stopped since, professional as ever."

The old man started dealing out tin plates of apple pie. Stringer dug into his. It was warm, but sort of tasteless. He said it was the best apple pie he'd ever had. He turned to Deputy Jacobs after swallowing a second mouthful. "I can see why you'd suspect those slippery trainrobbers of doubling back after laying a false scent clear out of these United

States. But how come you think they could be hiding out in Iron Mountain of all places? You could pitch horseshoes with the stakes set at the city limits, either way. There can't be more than a few dozen folk, living there regular, and I was just allowed to observe that they don't welcome strangers with open arms up there," Stringer said.

"I know the place," Jacobs replied. "You're right. We don't expect to find Butch or Sundance there. But we got a tip that Etta Place could be laying low in Iron Mountain."

Stringer laughed, louder than he felt like laughing, and asked, "Doing what? There's a general store with an attached saloon and, oh, yeah, a blacksmith. The rest of the town consists of bitty cabins. I'm sure someone would have mentioned it to me if a lady bandit had robbed a chicken coop in recent memory."

Jacobs coughed up some apple pie. "Miss Etta ain't exactly a lady bandit. She's more the lady love of the Sundance Kid. With the gang scattered and laying low, she could be getting money by mail from her outlaw lover. We'll ask her, when we catch her."

Stringer swallowed some pie that suddenly tasted even drier in his mouth and washed it down with coffee that refused to taste wet. "Well, I was only in town a short spell," he said, "but it's a mighty short town and I'd say I must have at least nodded to everyone there by now. What does this Etta Place look like, Deputy?"

"Pretty and sort of refined," Jacobs said, "considering the company she keeps. It's easy to see how that story about her being a wayward schoolmarm or a runaway society gal got started. Her exact age is up for grabs, since Etta Place is hardly the name she'd have on any birth certificate. But she looks to be in her middle twenties, with a fine figure and brown hair."

"How dark a head of hair are we talking about?" asked Stringer.

Jacobs said, "Oh, just a regular brown, neither amazingly light or dark. Why do you ask?"

"I thought I might have had something for you. But it don't work. The only gal I spotted up yonder that fits at all was cheap, flashy, and had jet black hair. I suspect she's a breed. They call her Cherokee."

"Do tell? What was she doing while anyone was looking?"

Stringer shot a wary look at the old lady by the stove, winked at Jacobs, then confided, "About what you'd expect a flashy sass like that to be doing in a cow town."

Jacobs lowered his voice. "You mean, selling charms to the local boys?" he asked.

Stringer's code forebade him to kiss and tell unless it was in a good cause. Since he owed the gal, he grinned sort of dirty and said, "I can't speak for *all* the local boys. But *I* got some, if that's what you're asking."

Jacobs grimaced in distaste and muttered, "Keep your fool voice down. Are you sure that... breed was called Cherokee?"

Stringer shrugged and said, "That's what she *said* I could call her, why?"

Jacobs sighed, "That's the handle our informant gave us. Black hair, you say, and acting that common?" He turned to one of his men to ask, "What do you think, Bob?"

The other lawman shook his head and said, "Might look like Etta Place. Can't see the real one acting like so. Sundance would skin her and any man he caught with her alive. He ain't as good-natured as Butch."

Jacobs turned back to Stringer, stared at him for a long unwinking moment, then said, "I don't recall your face on any wanted posters. But just the same, would you mind showing us some I.D., friend?"

Stringer gladly hauled out his press credentials. Jacobs scanned them and handed them back, saying, "I think I've read your stuff in the papers, Mister MacKail. So far, I've never caught you in a serious mistake. What were you doing up in Iron Mountain to begin with?"

Stringer explained his interest in Tom Horn's case. Jacobs looked pained and said, "I wish they'd just hang that fool and shut him up for good. Men who live by dealing death ought to be man enough to face death when it's dealt to them."

"Do you think he's really guilty as charged?"

"Quien sabe? If Joe LeFors framed him, it was in a good cause. Like I said, Tom Horn's a born killer who should have been hung years ago."

Stringer sipped more coffee. It tasted wetter now. Then he asked, "What would you call Deputy Marshal LeFors, if he's sending an innocent man to the gallows?"

Jacobs growled, "Don't try to put words in my mouth, newspaper man. I'd be willing to say it to Joe's face that I don't like him. He ain't an easy man to like. But I've never caught him in an outright lie and he did swear under oath that Tom Horn confessed that killing to him."

"Tom Horn swears he didn't. That he was too drunk at the time to string words together sensible. Yet the confession Joe LeFors read to the court was not only coherent but worded in correct English Tom Horn can't even manage sober."

Jacobs shrugged. "Mebbe old Joe saw fit to punctuate more proper. Mebbe Horn was confessing some other killing he'd had a hand in. Mebbe, like Horn says, LeFors just figured it was time to arrest a known killer one damn way or another. Who cares?"

"Nobody but me and Tom Horn, I fear," Stringer sighed.

Jacobs said, "There you go. Look on the bright side. It ain't you they's fixing to hang. That storm outside sounds like it's letting up a mite. Finish your coffee and you can ride back to Cheyenne with us."

Stringer felt so smart he wanted to hug himself. But he looked innocent and asked, "Oh? I thought you boys meant to push on to Iron Mountain."

"In this rain, on a wild goose chase?" Jacobs said. "We'll likely drown getting back to Cheyenne as it is. But thanks to you, we don't have to get any wetter."

The one called Bob grinned dirty and said, "Oh, I don't know. It might be fun to question that breed gal personal, seeing she's so friendly."

Jacobs laughed. "She's got plenty of sisters in sin back in town if you're feeling romantic enough to ride through a storm for such conversations, Bob."

"You're right," Bob said. "Let's go find some. But first I mean to hunt down that informer and give him a good licking for soaking me half to death with that bum steer about Etta Place. How do you suppose he ever got her mixed up with a flashy no-good breed?"

"Easy," Jacobs replied. "He wanted drinking money and so he just sort of described a trail town tramp that sort of fit. Think how sore you'd be if we'd ridden all that way for nothing."

CHAPTER
SEVEN

The summer storm had blown over by the time Stringer was back at the Drover's Palace. Despite his slicker, he couldn't really tell until he'd enjoyed a hot tub bath and changed into dry duds and socks. Old Jim Tate had been right about the draws flooding saddle-swell deep, and wind atop the rises had fired raindrops point blank and even up at them.

The city of Cheyenne was still dripping some under a clear gloaming sky when Stringer looked Bat Masterson up at his own hotel a few streets over. The older newspaperman had changed his own socks, he said, as they gathered in the tap room downstairs to compare notes. He said, "I ran for it with everyone else when the thunderbird commenced to poop. But I wasn't able to catch a cab, and by the time I made her back to town the streets were ankle deep, curb to curb. It was fun, carrying ladies over the roaring rapids—that is, once I decided there was no way to get any wetter."

Stringer clinked beer schooners with him and said,

"When it rains on the High Plains it makes up for the dust all at once. I hope you took notes for the two of us before the sporting events were called on account of rain?"

"Nope. Didn't get the chance," Masterson replied. "The storm washed today's show out before it could get started. Put the main events a day behind schedule. But I don't think the local merchants are all that upset. Just about everyone in the world seems to be here in Cheyenne right now and the longer they stay the more money they figure to spend. How come you got back so soon, Stringer? I figured you'd be up north until the closing ceremonies."

"I almost wound up staying longer," Stringer said, bringing Masterson up to date on his shoot-out with the late Billy Gower and its fortunate aftermath.

The older man whistled and said, "I thought I'd heard the last of such bullshit when I turned in my badge. Billy Gower is a new name to me. They must have raised a whole new generation of the breed since my bullet-ducking days."

Stringer asked, "Did you ever meet Deputy Marshal Joe LeFors? He's about your age, no offense, so he has to go back a ways."

Masterson sipped some suds while he did his thinking. Then nodding, he said, "I knew a Joe LeFors in Dodge well enough to howdy. I can't say it was the same one, though. I sort of kept an eye on his gun hand while I waited for him to howdy back. He wasn't working for the law in Dodge. Some said he was just a good old boy who packed all that artillery lest the gals who worked for Madame Moustache scalp him. Others said he was a hired gun. I never had any trouble with him. So I just can't say."

Stringer said, "LeFors is an unusual name to begin with and they'd hardly all be named Joseph after that. So the name, the age, and the rep all fit. You're not the first to opine that the gent's sort of sinister, no matter what Uncle Sam and the Union Pacific think of him right now. Tom Horn says LeFors swore false testimony against him in court. Today I talked to other lawmen who consider it possible."

Bat Masterson looked pained. "If I were you I'd drop her, Stringer. I wasn't there neither, but I did read up on the trial. Somewhere in the small print it said the arresting officer had a secretary taking down Horn's confession in that saloon, whether it was in Omaha or here in Cheyenne. You can't expect the papers to pick all the nits."

"Oh, sure," Stringer said, "I can just see Tom Horn dictating slow enough for a stenographer as all three of them swill booze together in a saloon. Meanwhile, not one witness put Tom Horn anywhere in Laramie County at the time that Nickell boy was shot. A mess of witnesses saw James Miller stab his father less than six months earlier, and not one was asked to testify at Tom Horn's trial. Wouldn't you say that was pretty raw, Bat?"

"Yep. But that's the way a lot of this country got cleaned up, kid. We're not talking about a virgin school marm being framed for swiping apples. Some say the trial of Henry McArthy, Kid Antrim, Billy the Kid or whatever you want to call the murderous little bastard was based on the sworn testimony of his sworn enemies. But there's no getting around the fact that the Kid openly boasted of killing twenty-one men and might have really murdered as many as five or six. What were they supposed to do, let him off, just because they couldn't prove some of the minor details?"

"That's the way the Constitution reads, Bat."

"Yeah, well, them old gents in white wigs who writ it never could have imagined what things would be like out here after Sam Colt made every man equal indeed. Rough justice is better than none in rough country, old son. Look how the Kid acted even after all them sob sisters wrote him up as a misguided youth who never meant no harm. Whether his trial was fair or not, didn't he kill two deputies busting out of jail and didn't old Pat Garrett do the right thing by him when they met up at the Maxwell spread a short time later?"

Stringer grimaced. "We were talking about Tom Horn. Joe LeFors never shot it out with a man who thought he was a friend. He got him too drunk to fight that virgin schoolmarm you just mentioned and let him wake up in jail, charged with a confession Horn just can't remember making."

"Don't let this get around, lest Ned Buntline turn over in his grave, but there are times a lawman has to take a bad man as best he can. It just ain't true, or sensible, that the law owes an outlaw an even break. I don't know how good this Joe LeFors might be. But Tom Horn could beat nine out of ten mortal men in a sober quick-draw contest. So what was LeFors supposed to do, walk up to Tom Horn like a big ass bird and say, 'Howdy, you're under arrest for a hanging offense and I sure hope you'll come quiet?'" Masterson asked.

"If he'd done that, they'd have had one hell of a time convicting Horn of anything, even if he had come quiet," Stringer replied.

"I know," Masterson said. "That's doubtless why they took him sort of dirty. Every time in the past the law saw fit to question him about a killing, Tom Horn got off for lack of evidence. It's a pure bitch to hang a killing on a gent when it takes place far from civilization, man-to-man on the lone prairie. As an old Apache scout, Tom Horn left no sign for anyone to read. It's a cruel fact of nature that when the law can't get anything on an owlhoot it just has to make something up. You're wasting your time, Stringer. Even if you could find some evidence clearing Horn of the Nickell killing, Wyoming has made her mind up to hang the poor bastard and that's all there is to it. You couldn't get him off with you and Teddy Roosevelt swearin' on a stack of Bibles that he was playing cards with you at the time Wyoming says he murdered that boy."

Stringer brightened. "I met President Roosevelt just a while ago and Tom Horn served with the Rough Riders in Cuba."

"Forget it," Masterson said. "Old Teddy is a politician and the voters of Wyoming want to see Horn swing. He'd never pardon another outlaw now, even if Wyoming wanted him to. He still hasn't lived Henry Starr down yet."

Stringer asked what they were talking about and Masterson explained. "Starr's an Oklahoma breed some say could be kin to Sam Starr, the Cherokee husband of the Belle called the same. Following the family trade, young Henry stuck up as many as forty small-town banks before he got into a shoot-out with Deputy U.S. Marshal Floyd Wilson, killed him dead as a turd in a milk bucket, and was sentenced to hang for the deed. The Cherokee Tribal Council raised such a fuss about it that Teddy Roosevelt stepped in and pardoned him. Don't ask me how they convinced Teddy he was acting rational. Suffice it to say that less than a month after they let him out, Henry Starr held up the bank of Bentonville, Arkansas, got away clean with the contents of the vault, and is still at large. I don't think this would be a good time to ask a mighty pissed-off president to pardon another western outlaw for old time's sake."

Stringer sighed. "Oh, well, Horn told me that if the boys he was with somewhere else at the time don't come forward to save him he means to tell it all to the papers on his own. You may be right. I'd say I've done about as much as anyone on our side of the law could be expected to on his behalf."

When he finished his beer Masterson asked if Stringer'd like another. "No, thanks," Stringer answered. "While it's still early I thought I'd mosey over to the fair grounds and catch up on the job I was sent here to do. In a way that unexpected rain may have done me a favor. Aside from giving me extra time to cover the rodeo, it seems to have cooled my head a mite."

He rose from the table. Bat Masterson said he didn't want to get his fresh socks wet again but walked with him to the side entrance leading to the street. As they stepped out to shake and part friendly, Masterson suddenly pushed Stringer one way and moved the other, reaching under his frock coat as a rifle round whizzed through the space they'd just been standing in and showered them both with pulverized brick!

Stringer got behind a cast iron watering trough as Masterson took cover behind a parked electric delivery van, snapping, "On the roof across the way. I spotted the glint of sunset on gun-metal just in time. Once you've seen it you never forget. What do we do now?"

Stringer said, "Make 'em work at it. I'll cover while you duck back inside."

Masterson didn't argue. He said, "Now!" and moved with surprising speed for a man his age, running in a crouch. Stringer didn't spot any movement along the skyline across the way until he heard Masterson call out from the doorway, "I've got that rooftop in my sights now, boy. Move your skinny ass!"

Stringer did so. As he whipped by the older man in his own low run Masterson swung the door shut and waited for Stringer to stop skidding on his boot heels across the waxed and sawdust-covered floor before he heaved a great sigh and said, "I told you the whole damned world seemed to be in Cheyenne this evening. But that couldn't have been Billy the Kid, even if he did favor such methods."

The other gents who'd been drinking in the tap room were on their feet now. The barkeep yelled a plaintive request for more information about all that unseemly behavior. Stringer rejoined Masterson by the door, saying, "Someone pegged a shot our way just now. It seems to be over, for now."

That didn't seem to be good enough for some of the other patrons of the bar. They left via the exit to the hotel lobby. The barkeep swore and started taking down the mirror from the wall behind the bar. He'd no sooner done so when someone began to pound the side door officiously. Masterson said, "I'd say that was a billy club," and opened the door a crack. Then he nodded to admit the two Cheyenne beat coppers. They naturally demanded to know who might be responsible for all that noise they'd just heard.

"It wasn't us," Stringer said. "You can sniff our gun barrels if you like."

The senior officer protested he was the law, not a durned old dawg, and asked the barkeep's opinion. The man they knew and trusted, bless him, said, "That gent in the derby hat is a guest at this hotel. Don't know the one dressed cow. But the two of them was drinking civilized in here up to a moment ago. Then they tried to leave by that door you just came in by and I heard a shot from outside. I can't say it surprised me to see them two whip back inside. I'd say they were telling it true."

The senior officer told Stringer and Bat Masterson to put their durned guns away and opined, "Might have been a drunk, shooting wild. We caught a gent this afternoon lobbing quarter-sticks of dynamite out his hotel window.

He was too drunk to explain just why he thought that was so funny. Do either of you gents have cause to think anyone could be after you, personal?"

Bat Masterson stared curiously at Stringer, who shrugged and said, "We're both newspapermen, here for your Frontier Days. We hardly know anyone here in Cheyenne."

It worked. They said they'd have a look around the neighborhood and left to get back to their own drinking. Masterson told Stringer, "It's not my fight. But if I were you, I'd have let the law in on it, son."

"Until I know just where the law stands in this town I'll feel safer doing my own fighting," Stringer replied. "I thought it was over. And it would be, if the bastards would only leave me alone. But since they won't, it ain't, and now I'm really starting to get pissed."

Bat Masterson had been right about the fair grounds being muddy. It wasn't so bad once you got your boots on the tanbark, though. That was one of the reasons they spread it in the first place. It was still light enough to see where he was going and he found Miss Rimfire Rowena over by the chutes, jawing with what looked like an upright grizzly bear until Stringer got close enough to see it was a big burly colored man in a coffee brown shirt and brown wool chaps. As he joined them Rimfire Rowena said, "Meet Bill Pickett from Texas, MacKail. He just got here and where have you been all this time?"

Stringer shook hands with Pickett as he told her, "Chasing rainbows and getting rained on. I've met Bill here, before. I doubt he'd remember. I was just a kid when my Uncle Don introduced us out Frisco way."

The bearlike colored hand grinned and said, "If your uncle would be Don MacKail from Calaveras County, I do remember you and you're right, you've grown some. What might you be entered in, the saddle broncs or the roping?"

"Neither. I'm covering all the events as a stringer for the *San Francisco Sun*. That's why they call me Stringer these days, Bill. Which event are you entered in, as if I have to ask?"

The husky black, or as some said, half black and half Indian, smiled sheepishly and said, "Anything but roping. I rope as good as the regular job calls for, I reckon. But some of the tricks they do with ropes these days don't look possible. Have you ever seen Will Rogers spin a rope, Stringer?"

"Not in any rodeo, if we're talking about the same stage-show performer. They had a Will Rogers on the bill with Eddy Foy the last time I was in Denver. Could we be talking about the same young gent?"

Pickett nodded. "We could. Young Will and me rode together a spell for the old 101 Spread. He was an Oklahoma breed, only white where he wasn't Cherokee, so we got sort of close. He was a good cowhand and a roper you had to see to believe. He used to get hell from the ramrod for roping so showboat whilst we was supposed to be branding. Old Will just could not or would not rope a calf natural. He'd throw loops looked like figure eights or butterflies or, hell, squares and triangles when he was really having fun. When they fussed at him for being so silly he'd call his shots, like a pool shark, and rope one leg, two, or all four. Killed a range bull one time, busting it by the forelegs just for fun. When they fired him he run off to the Boer War, riding for the Boers, of course, and then when him and another young cowhand called Tom Mix got deported back to the States by the winning side, he went into show business. I'm sort of sorry he ain't here to enter the roping events tomorrow. He'd win, sure, and the entrance fees get bigger every season."

Rimfire Rowena said, "That's what we was just thinking about, MacKail. As a performing artist I don't have to put up no prize money. They pay me a flat fee to perform, see—not even the one and original Annie Oakley dares to face me in a fair shooting match. But some of the boys have been hard put to scrape up the entrance fees they're asking, here."

"Oh? What kind of money are we talking?" Stringer asked.

"It depends on the event and the prizes," Bill Pickett explained. "I reckon it's fair enough. The prizes get bigger every year and it's established custom to make up the winner's purse from the entrance fees of the losers."

Rimfire Rowena said, "I don't think it's fair. It seems to me they ought to pay everyone, win or lose. I know I'd never get bucked on my fool head for nothing, and if nobody ever lost, how much of a show would they have to offer in the first damn place?"

"Now, Miss Rowena," Bill Pickett said, "they have to charge an entrance fee. If they didn't, every fool kid in the country would want to ride. By making a rider put his money where his mouth is, they weed out all but the serious gents. Ain't that right, Stringer?"

Stringer shrugged. "There's much to be said for both your points of view. They'd have a time awarding enough prize money to matter if they just took it out of the tickets to the show. The promoters who set these contests up must feel they're entitled to some profit. It's just as true that asking a rider to bet money on his own skills tends to separate the men from the boys. But, on the other hand, I see Miss Rowena's point that it's asking a lot of a man to go home broke as well as busted up with doctor bills if he takes a bad fall."

Rimfire Rowena said, "Oh, they ain't that mean, here. I heard some of the committee arguing that point this morning, before the show was called on account of rain and they was still waiting for it to start."

Both men stared down at her with the same unspoken question. So she explained, "The out-of-towners who organized the show seem to think that a man dumb enough to get hurt should pay his own fool doctor bills. But the townees who agreed to let 'em hold the show here seemed to take a different view. This one old gent was saying that since the town of Cheyenne could get stuck with unpaid hospital bills if anyone got hurt real bad, the promoters ought to set aside a medical fund to make sure anyone in the show or just up in the stands could get proper attention if they needed it. He was a nice old gent, for a townee. I think they said he was some sort of judge when he wasn't judging contests."

Stringer asked, "Could his name have been Judge Kenton?"

Rimfire Rowena replied, "As a matter of fact it was. Do you know him?"

"Yeah," Stringer said, nodding. "My lawyer told me he was a decent gent, too. I hope he knows as much about judging riders as he does about common law. He was on the money with that suggestion about a medical fund. The promoters could be long gone by the time anyone gets around to suing for damages, and he was right when he said the city couldn't just leave a busted-up rider or spectator to die of neglect."

He turned to Bill Pickett, patting him friendly on the back. "Speak up if you need a few bucks extra to get in, Bill. Since I know better than to carry on so foolishly I generally have a few cents change in my jeans."

The big black man looked touched. But he shook his

head and said, "Not hardly, thanks just the same. I finished in the money down at Lyons, just before I come up here. I can handle the entry fee. But I might look you up later, if I wind up feeling silly on the tanbark. Like I said, these days it seems to take the prize money from one rodeo just to make her to the next one. I wish I could go on the stage, like Will Rogers. But all the colored men they hire seem to be white boys with burnt cork smeared all over their fool faces. I don't know how to pluck a banjo anyhow."

Smiling, Stringer assured Pickett he could no doubt rake in the money at more honest work, then moved on to see if anyone else had something interesting to spill about the coming events.

Nobody he could find on the darkening fair grounds could tell him much more than he already knew. The rider called Slash said he didn't even want to talk to him. But when Stringer threatened to hit him some more, Slash grudgingly allowed he'd never heard of a Winfield Scott Rutherford or a Billy Gower and knew for a fact that neither was entered in any of the rodeo events past or future. Slash said he could read and that all the entrants were posted. And anyway, he was only interested in the saddle bronc event. So Stringer wished him luck and let him take leave with his face still intact.

Stringer found the bulletin board stuck to a shack between the chutes and the judges' stand. Neither was occupied at this hour, of course. Stringer got out his note pad and copied down the names of all the entrants. It might be interesting to see if all of them were still meaning to ride, or what anyone who failed to appear after posting an entry fee might look like. Billy Gower had been established as a gent who didn't always use his real name and he had been wearing a mighty fancy shirt when he died.

Having nosed about the fair grounds as much as he felt

up to, Stringer legged it back to town to see what sweet old Pat Morrison might be feeling up to. It was a mite early for slap and tickle. But since the evening was shaping up so warm and dry, she might just enjoy going out to dine first.

The notion inspired him to walk a mite faster. In no time at all he'd reached Pat's door and raised a fist to knock on it. But he never got to, because just then he heard a burst of loud laughter, male and female, coming from the far side.

As he lowered his fist Stringer swore at Pat and then had to laugh at himself. For while Pat had agreed to be his lawyer, she'd never sworn to be faithful about anything else, and he sure hadn't felt bound by any such considerations in the company of Cherokee, Etta Place, or whoever that sweet-screwing little gal might have been.

Stringer started to walk away, telling himself it was a free country. Then he slid into the slot between Pat's place and the next frame building over, even as he asked himself what in blue blazes he thought he was doing. Like most men, Stringer considered a Peeping Tom a contemptible idiot, unless it was him who was given the chance to peep. As he eased toward that side window he recalled from a happier occasion (with a certain bitterness he knew to be just dumb), he assured himself he had a right to make sure Pat wasn't plotting against him with whomever. He'd just have a little listen, and if all they were up to was fornication, he'd just be a sport about it and head back to his hotel. He might even forgive her, if there was anything at all attractive in the hotel tap rooms at this hour.

But when he got to the window he saw Pat's bedroom was too dark and too quiet for a gal who made love with her kind of enthusiasm. He shrugged and followed the slot toward the back alley. Pat's back fence was low, and if they were in the kitchen he could at least get a look at the son of a bitch who'd aced him out.

But just before he stepped out into the alley he froze at the sound of footsteps on wet gravel. They didn't sound like someone headed home the short way. They sounded like someone moving sneaky. So Stringer drew his .38 and waited to see what might happen next.

What happened next was that Friendly Frank Folsom, of all people, tried to pass Stringer's slot with an even bigger pistol in his right hand. He didn't get to. Stringer swung his own gun in an overhead arc and brought it down, hard, on the gunslick's forearm, breaking both bones, before he pistol-whipped what was left of Friendly Frank to the ground.

All things considered, Friendly Frank took it like a man, if a man was supposed to say all those mean things about Stringer's mother instead of outright weeping. As Friendly Frank tried to sit up, with his rump in a puddle, Stringer kicked him flat again, then bent down and took the other ivory-handled six-gun from its cussing owner. Then he sat on Friendly Frank's chest, put his own gun to Folsom's flustered face, and said, "If there is one thing I can't abide, it's a liar. You told me they hadn't offered you enough and that you meant to back off, you sneaky son of a two-faced bitch."

Friendly Frank groaned, "Jesus, you got one knee on my poor right arm and I fear it's already busted!"

Stringer poked him between the eyebrows with cold steel. "Unless you want to be put out of your misery, forever, we're going to hear some answers and they'd better be mighty convincing. I just caught you in one fib, Friendly Frank."

The helpless hired gun gapsed, "You're no-shit hurting me and I swear I wasn't after you just now, Stringer."

"That leaves only a lady then and whoever she seems fond of tonight. Which one did they send you to kill, and this time I really mean to find out just who *they* might be."

Friendly Frank said, "You got it all wrong. I'm more a sort of persuader than a killer, see?"

"Persuade me. Who sent you to do what?" Stringer asked.

"I was hired by a gent named Martin," Friendly Frank coughed out.

"Martin what?" Stringer pressed, waving his .38 too close for comfort.

The gunslick gasped. "Martin is his last name, not his first. I was told to just call him Mister Martin. He's some sort of businessman here in Cheyenne. That's all I really know about him, honest."

Stringer said, "Sure. Your Mister Martin just put an ad in the help-wanted section, saying he needed a hired gun, right?"

Friendly Frank sighed. "I was sort of referred to him by another gent in the trade. You'd have to ask him how him and Mister Martin got to know each other. I was sort of called in as extra help, when they noticed I was in town."

"All right," Stringer said. "So where do I find this murderous old pal of yours, old pal of mine?"

"He was staying at the Drover's Palace," Friendly Frank blurted out fast now. "That's how we knowed you was there. Since his face appears on more posters than mine, we figured it might be best if I was to be the one to run you off, see?"

"Not yet. How does this fellow guest of mine sign his own name, checking in?"

Friendly Frank explained, "He don't use his right name.

That could be a fatal mistake. He's using the name of Winfield Scott Rutherford these days."

Stringer swore and said, "I don't think I'd better tell you how I know you got those last orders direct from your Mister Martin this evening. But what were they?"

"Persuading," Friendly Frank said, "like I told you. Martin said I was to sort of lean on that lawyer gal, Patricia Morrison, and find out why you and her has gotten so thick. He said not to kill her or even rape her if I didn't have to, but to make it clear she was in for both if she didn't come clean about her business with you."

"He sounds like a swell gent," Stringer growled. "Just what did he want to know from my lawyer?"

"Ouch," Friendly Frank moaned when Stringer poked him in the gut again. "Exactly what the two of you was up to, of course. Martin seemed anxious to know if you was really serious about Tom Horn and if you'd found any evidence that might get him off. He said you had a rep for digging up the damndest things to print in your newspaper and that sometimes you played innocent until you was ready to spill all sorts of beans."

Stringer nodded grimly and asked, "What sort of beans do you reckon your Mister Martin might have that he don't want spilt?"

Friendly Frank groaned, "I honest to God don't know. Billy, I mean, Winfield Scott Rutherford knew him better than me. Why don't you ask him?"

"I'd sure like to," Stringer smirked. "What time is it?"

Friendly Frank looked startled. "Around nine, I suppose. Why do you ask?"

"There's a U.P. eastbound due in around nine-thirty. There won't be another train passing through until closer to midnight. So we'd best get cracking if we're to get you aboard that earlier one."

"But I don't have any call to board no eastbound train," Friendly Frank protested.

"Sure you do," Stringer said. "Let me help you up and get you to the depot. 'Cause if you miss that train, or ever come back here, I'm going to have to kill you. See?"

CHAPTER EIGHT

Considering how easy he was getting off, Friendly Frank sure bitched a lot about leaving town with a busted arm and no sidearms. When he asked what would happen if he met someone who might not like him before he could heal up and rearm, Stringer told him there was nothing—beast or man—could bring him worse disaster than showing his ugly face in Cheyenne for a spell.

After seeing the hired gun off at the depot, Stringer headed for the nearby Cheyenne Jail. He braced himself for another argument with that officious desk sergeant. But as luck would have it, a more easy-going cuss was on duty that night. When Stringer waved Judge Kenton's papers at him he just shrugged and said to leave any weapons he had with him at the desk. He whistled softly when Stringer lay his .38 and two ivory-handled .45s side by side and said, "Remind me never to get in an argument with such a grim friend of the court."

Then he whistled up a turnkey and locked Stringer tightly in with Tom Horn. The cell was almost pitch dark.

They were afraid to leave an oil lamp in there with him, according to Tom Horn. Stringer found that sort of cruel and unusual, even by Wyoming standards. So he ran an exploring hand along the wall near the door and, sure enough, fond an electric switch.

Tom Horn gasped and stared up in childlike wonder as the overhead Edison bulb flashed on, forty watts worth. "Well, I never," he gasped. "I've been wondering what that glass jar was doing stuck up there in the ceiling all this time. How did you get it to light up like that, pard?"

Stringer replied, "Judas Priest, Edison invented the electric light back in the seventies. Are you trying to say you never heard?"

Tom Horn shrugged and said, "Sure I did. I ain't ignorant. But to tell the truth I've spent more time out under the stars than in towns fancy enough to own electrical wonders. I've seen many an electrical light in my time, I reckon. Just never gave much thought to how they might work."

Stringer showed him how the switch worked by flicking the light off and on a few times. Tom Horn nodded gravely. "I sure thank you for illuminating me, Stringer. It was awfully morose sitting night after night in the dark from sundown to sunrise. But, listen, I got more important things to tell you. My old pards know where they can lay hands on some dynamite and..."

"Don't tell *me,* damnit," Stringer cut in, adding, with a sigh, "I'm packing papers making me a sort of court official and I was never an outlaw to begin with."

Horn declared, "Aw, I know I can trust *you.*"

"I hope that works both ways," Stringer said. "I rode up to Iron Mountain on your behalf. I didn't find out much. But someone tried to kill me just the same. Do you know a

Billy Gower or a man named Martin who might be interested in your case?"

"I know lots of Martins," Tom Horn said. "None that might have call to help or hurt me, though. I've heard tell of a Gower called Billy. Bad apple, if we're discussing the same idjet."

Stringer sat down beside Horn and rolled a smoke as he told the older man about his adventures up at Iron Mountain. When he got to the shoot-out with Gower, Horn cut in to opine, "That has to be the same idjet. Nobody with the brains of a gnat takes time to address a gent personal afore slapping leather on him. It may be safe to work yourself up to a fistfight. But when a man's out for real blood he's supposed to work hisself up afore he goes looking for his man. Gunfighting is a serious business. A man has no business even considering such an affair if he ain't dead certain to begin with that he really wants to kill somebody."

Stringer soothed, "Gower not doubt wasn't in the trade as long as you, Tom. I'd say we can both agree he had a lot to learn."

"Not no more," Horn chuckled. "I heard about him when he tried to sign on with the C.P.A. one time. They knew his rep and just laughed at him. He bragged that he'd already killed his man and more. But range detective is a skilled craft. You can't just ride about shooting tempting targets, just to be mean. I know they say mean things about the C.P.A. But the big cattlemen only want real cow thieves and such shot."

Stringer struck a light for his Bull Durham and got it going before he said, "That's the way I read her when I had a look at where Willie Nickell died, Tom. The killing never did any cattle baron a lick of good. Both the Nickells and Millers still own their fenced-in spreads and both clans still range some of their stock on public land. If killing that kid was meant to run anyone off their homesteads, it didn't work worth a damn and we're talking a couple of summers ago."

"I know," Horn said. "The boy'd been dead and buried almost two years afore they arrested me for it, and damnit, I was way the hell up north, persuading a fence-stringing pest of the error of his ways."

Stringer blew a smoke ring. "Tom. Rehashing the facts everyone knows isn't about to do you any good at this late date. I've done all I can for you, with the bare bones you gave me to work with. You have to give me the names of those other hired guns who were with you when Willie Nickell was bushwhacked."

Horn shook his head and said, "No, I don't. Like I said, they just got in touch with me. I knew they wouldn't let a friend down. You was right about them not wanting to go to jail with me over some harmless fun with wire cutters and coal oil. But they have a plan to get me out, the easy way, see?"

Stringer looked real unhappy. "At the risk of aiding and abetting, I have to tell you what I think of such plans. Getting you to try a fool jailbreak could be a mighty slick way of shutting you up for good. We've already established that someone's ready and willing to kill me lest I stumble over one morsel of evidence that might win you an appeal. It seems to me that if the gents who claim to be your pards were at all sincere, they'd be rooting for me instead of shooting at me."

Horn insisted stubbornly, "I told you Billy Gower was never on the same payroll as me. Maybe it's Joe LeFors who don't want you proving what a big fibber he was in court."

"I've considered that," Stringer said sharply. "Deputy Marshal LeFors is hundreds of miles from here. But anything's possible. Meanwhile, you're still fixing to get killed and solve the problem for whomever, if you go messing with dynamite in a cell this size."

Tom Horn reached under his mattress as he smirked and told Stringer, "That goes off outside, just enough to crumble the back wall of this brick box. Look what they smuggled in for me to use more personal."

Stringer repressed a shiver as the old, dumb, and deadly man produced a wickedly efficient 9mm automatic pistol. "I wish you hadn't shown me that, Tom."

"I had to," Horn replied. "You're more educated about modern notions than me. I've been fooling and fooling with the infernal machine and you got to show me how it works."

Stringer gulped and said, "It looks like one of those new Luger automatics, Tom, American design and German manufacture."

Horn said, "I know. It says so, on the side, here. I got the clip figured. You slide her in and out with this bitty steel button. This other doohickey seems to be the safety switch and I've tried with it on and off. What I can't seem to work out is how in thunder you get a round in the damned chamber. Each time I hauls the clip out, it's got the same nine rounds in it. I've tried to dry-fire her with the clip out, but I can't get a peep outten the hammer, if it *has* a damned old hammer. They got all the innards hid inside. I sure wish they'd slipped a plain six-gun in to me."

Stringer asked mildly, "I don't suppose it's occurred to you that someone might have wanted you out of your depth with a gun in your hand?"

"Hell," Horn insisted, "them bullets are real enough and I've been assured this modernistic nine-shooter spits quicker and straighter than any gun I'm likely to go up against in these parts. It seems to me that if you pull back on these twin knobs above the trigger it ought to slide the action back and forth around in the chamber. But pull as I might, I can't get 'em to budge. Do you know what I'm doing wrong?"

Stringer did. The action of a Luger was tricky indeed and the way to work it called for pulling the loading knobs straight up, not backwards or forwards. The ingenious action worked by jackknifing rather than sliding, as one might expect. He said, "I've never owned a Luger, Tom." Which was the simple truth when one studied on it.

Horn handed him the stubborn if deadly weapon and suggested he give it a try. Stringer hauled straight back, and when—naturally—nothing happened, he said, "You'd better not try to throw down anyone with this, Tom. A gun you can't fire is worse than no gun at all. It gives all sorts of gents a good excuse to shoot you. It could be embarrassing as hell."

Horn took the weapon back, fiddled with the stubborn knobs until he got one finger to bleed, then said, "Well, I'll feel just as embarrassed standing there with a noose around my neck. So I'll just have to study on her some more." Then he hid the Luger away again.

They went on talking until Stringer had smoked down to nothing worth another drag. Then, since they still hadn't settled anything, Stringer stomped out what was left and got back to his feet. "I've done all I can if you won't give me any more leads, Tom," he said. "I hope you'll tell your pals that for me. I'd hate to wind up dead by mistake. As of now, you're all theirs, you poor trusting soul."

Back at his hotel, Stringer borrowed the city directory and sat down across the lobby to read it by the light of an India rubber plant. Martin was not quite as common a name as Smith or Jones. But it was common enough. He found a page and a half of Martins, and Cheyenne wasn't near as big as Frisco.

Three of them were listed as doctors and four as lawyers. It didn't say what all those other Cheyenne Martins did for a living. It was getting sort of late to call on lawyers at home with a tale at least three of them might find crazy enough to report to the law. To begin with any Martin interested in the life or death of a range detective was more likely to be a cattleman, and to begin even *more* with, the Mr. Martin that Friendly Frank had confessed to knowing would have been a fool to use his real name for hiring professionals to send after folk. This world was filled with fools. But better let the lawyer Martins off. Lawyers knew more than most about covering their tracks.

Stringer rose, gave the directory back to the desk clerk, and strolled into the tap room to see if any Gibson Girl wanted him to buy her some Coca-Cola. The stuff had lost most of its kick since Teddy Roosevelt had ordered them to stop putting cocaine in it. But Gibson Girls still sipped it, feeling up to date and sort of naughty.

He failed to see a Gibson or any other kind of girl in the half-deserted tap room. He ordered a beer, not wanting to feel naughty all by himself, and carried it to a secluded corner booth. Then he got out his notes and went over the list of rodeo contestants he'd taken down, more thoughtfully this time. He recognized some of the names. Rodeo riding was getting to be a regular sport now, just like baseball. He didn't see any Martins or Smiths, and he knew Buck Jones was a real cowhand—mighty young to be entered in the saddle broncs, but if his momma didn't care it was nobody else's business. None of the names Stringer failed to recognize matched any sinister reps he'd heard about in his travels. He decided to keep the list handy and check off each name as its owner came out of the chutes or failed to. He knew it was a long shot. For despite his taste in shirts, it hardly figured that Billy Gower would want to shoot men for money if he felt sure enough about his roping or riding to put up a stiff entrance fee.

Stringer put the list away and slowly sipped beer until there was no more left. He considered ordering another. Then he got up, yawned, and decided a good night's sleep, alone, wouldn't kill him. He was still a mite saddle sore from all that cross-country riding and he hadn't rested his legs much since getting back to town.

But as he was passing the desk the clerk called out, "I just now got a telephone message for you, Mister MacKail. I didn't know you were next door. So I told the lady you weren't here."

Stringer frowned and said, "A lady, you say? What was her name?"

The clerk replied, "She didn't leave her name. Just a number for you to call. Would you rather call from down here or up in your room?"

Stringer said there was little sense in climbing two flights of stairs if he might be going out some more. So the clerk shot him a knowing look and told him to pick up the desk set. Then he stepped back to the hotel switchboard and put the call through for Stringer. It rang three times at the far end. Then a pissed-off female voice was asking him, "Where have you been all this time, damnit?"

Stringer sighed and said, "I can see you found out I was back in town. When I called on you earlier, you seemed sort of busy with someone else. So I thought it best to just move on."

"Are you crazy?" she snapped. "What ever made you think I had something wicked going on with him? We're just good friends, you fool. Where have you been all this time? Was she pretty?"

He laughed and said, "Jealousy sure sounds dumb, coming from someone else. But I know the feeling. So let's just say we're even and let it go at that. I can only think of one way to assure you I haven't been with another woman tonight. So prepare to meet your maker as soon as I can get over there and ride you to glory, you pretty little thing."

She gasped and replied, "You sure come right to the point. But aren't you taking a lot for granted, you brute?"

He sighed. "Oh, come on, are you one of those gals who expects a man to start courting from scratch every time he wants to go to bed with you? I would have offered to take you out on the town earlier if you hadn't been jawing with that other gent. But you were, and I'm sorry if I took it wrong. The point is that it's too late now. I'm tired after a long hard day, but I may be able to rise to the occasion if we can get right down to it. So do you want me to come over or don't you?"

There was a long thoughtful silence. Then she sighed and said, "You're just so damned romantic I'd be a fool to resist you. But I don't want to meet you at my ... ah ... public address. You know how people talk. I've taken a hotel room in town for the night. I'm at the Laramie Hotel, just down the street from you. Do you think you can find it, honey bunch?"

He growled, "Not if you call me honey bunch when I get there. What room number shall I ask for, doll face?"

She said, "I'm in 202 but don't ask. I checked in alone. It's a big old hotel with four ways into the lobby. Just walk in like you own the place and come on up. You won't find the door locked and if you want..."

"Hold on," he stopped her. "I know it's none of my business. But about that other gent you were entertaining earlier..."

She sounded flustered, perhaps hiding something, as she told him, "Didn't you even look at him? I wasn't entertaining him. We were just talking, about the rodeo tomorrow, dear."

"How come?" he asked. "You're not riding in any fool rodeo, are you?"

"Of course not," she giggled. "But he is. Can't we talk about it later, I mean, *soon?*"

He laughed, hung up, and left the brace of guns he'd taken from Friendly Frank with the desk clerk for safekeeping. He might have left his .38 as well—had he been feeling safe at all. But while at least two gunslicks of the mysterious Mr. Martin had been accounted for, Mr. Martin was still in town and such help came cheap. He'd make up his mind about the rodeo rider Pat had been entertaining in her kitchen *after* he heard her explain a little better just what in thunder a gent like that needed with a lady lawyer if the lady was only feeling platonic about him.

The streets were darker and less crowded now. He ran the odd conversation through again a few times as he legged it towards her hotel. Whatever a rodeo rider might have wanted at her place, Friendly Frank wouldn't have been creeping up on the two of them if Pat's mystery guest had been in on it with the mysterious Mr. Martin. He was likely just a would-be client and Pat was right about how easy it was to take male visitors after dark the wrong way. He'd been guilty of such hasty conclusions himself.

But wasn't it a mite late for old Pat to commence worrying about what the neighbors might think? She hadn't worried about that other male visitor laughing like a jackass loud enough to be heard through closed doors. She hadn't worried about hauling a client into bed the night before last, with that open side window broadcasting her moaning and groaning to just about anyone with an ear for listening.

Stringer slowed his pace as he spied the sign of her hotel ahead. He tried to decide whether it made good sense for a lady with her own private quarters to check into a downtown hotel if it was just privacy she was wanting. He tried to decide if that had really been her voice on the telephone. You got to where you could tell, after you'd talked to the same person a few times through an electric wire. But he'd never talked to Pat on any telephone—before now.

He moved on, entered the Laramie Hotel via a side entrance, and put a silver dollar on the marble desktop, telling the bemused clerk on duty, "I'll bet you a dollar you don't know how to let me make a telephone call to some friends of mine here in town."

The clerk scooped the coin up, saying, "You lose. What number do you want us to connect you to?"

Stringer swore softly as he realized he hadn't picked up that message slip from the other desk clerk. Then he brightened, asked to see their city directory, and had no trouble finding Pat's telephone number listed next to her name and address. The clerk told him to use the second set down the desk, wrote the number on yet another slip, and passed it back to the switchboard gal.

This time it rang a dozen times before Stringer decided Pat was really upstairs in 202 like she'd said. But just as he was about to hang up, someone picked up at the far end and he heard a much more familiar voice moan, "What on earth do you want? We'd just fallen to sleep. I mean, I just went to sleep and who is this?"

Stringer didn't feel like a long tedious conversation with a gal in bed with another man. So he just hung up. He nodded his thanks and moved away from the desk, feeling more confused than sore. It was small wonder that other gal had sounded a mite mixed up in places. She'd been making answers up as they went along.

He moved toward the front entrance, keeping a wary eye on all the rubber plants. He tensed, then relaxed as he recognized Bat Masterson and another gent coming in off the street.

Masterson greeted him with, "Howdy, kid. Meet a pal and fellow writer of ours, Charlie Siringo. Like me, he was a lawman before he saw the light."

As Stringer shook with the distinguished older man, he said, "I read your *Texas Cowboy*, Mister Siringo. Was it meant to be fact or fiction?"

The old-timer laughed lightly. "A little of both, I reckon. We all know how editors like to liven things up. Call me Charlie and, unlike Bat, here, I ain't sold enough yet to call myself a full-time writer. I spent more time learning riding than reading and writing, growing up in Texas after my daddy got here from Italy, so I have to write careful and slow. Meanwhile, I'm still with Pinkerton. Can't say I like it, but a man has to eat."

Bat Masterson said, "Pay him no mind. He may write slow but I wish I could write half as good. What are you doing here at Charlie's hotel, Stringer?"

Stringer replied, "I was about to walk into a trap until I caught on." Then he told the two old-timers about the tempting telephone call and they agreed perfidity had to be the name of woman until a better one came along.

Bat Masterson asked how Stringer meant to cope with the setup and was told, "I was about to mosey out the door and start running. I'm not sure where. I can't go back to my own hotel or anywhere else they might know about here in Cheyenne."

Bat Masterson agreed he was in a fix. Old Charlie Siringo said, "Hell, what are we jawing about? Let's take 'em out."

Masterson cautioned, "Now, Charlie, didn't you just tell me you were only passing through?"

The crusty Texan replied, "That's another reason not to shilly-shally. I got a late night train to catch. Run the whole setup past us again, kid."

Stringer did. It was Masterson who decided, "If they was set up to bushwhack him down here in the lobby we wouldn't be talking about it this late. Stairwell?"

Siringo shook his head and said, "Risky, considering all the safer ways to do her. I know where 202 figures to be. Numbers run the same on my floor, higher up. It's a corner room. Anyone pounding on that door is exposed to the length of two corridors."

Masterson said, "Right. He knocks, someone pops out another door, either way, and just makes for a graceful exit after the kid here hits the rug full of lead."

Stringer asked, "Why couldn't they be planning on getting me from inside—as the bait invites me in?"

The two older men exchanged disgusted looks. Masterson said, "They could indeed, but then the law would no doubt want a word with the lady who booked that room. Disguises and false names work better in mystery stories than real life. On the other hand, what call would the law have to question a lady whose only crime was noticing you lay dead in the hallway sort of near her door? Every dead man in a hallway has to wind up near some damned door. She could just say she had no notion at all as to who such a disgusting sight might be and . . ."

"Never mind, I get the picture," Stringer cut in, going on to ask, "What do you gents reckon we can do about it?"

Siringo said, "Well, it's always best to take at least some damned body alive. The bait sounds easy enough.

We'll go up together and then spread out. I'll cover you the length of one corridor and Bat, here, can cover you the other way. Then you only have to bang on that door and announce yourself in a manly tone. Out of line from a shot through the door panels, of course. If any other doors pop open, me or Bat, depending, can freeze or smoke the popper in our own sweet way. Meanwhile, you bust in on the bait, shove your gun in her face, and see what she has to say."

Stringer asked, "What if she says I'm dead? What if I bust into a firing squad on the far side of that door?"

The grim old Pinkerton man told him, "We'll have 'em boxed-in, and you can rest assured Bat and me will avenge you a heap."

Stringer said he'd think about it on the way upstairs. But by the time they'd made it to the second floor he hadn't come up with anything better. So he sighed and said, "All right, it's my funeral. I'm just as likely to wind up dead some other way, if I can't catch someone who knows what's going on and make him or her talk."

Neither of the older gunslicks answered, both running off to take up their positions eagerly as hunting dogs, or perhaps a couple of old timber wolves that hadn't tasted blood for a spell.

Stringer waited until he was well covered from both angles. Then he drew his .38, took a deep breath, and knocked on the door of room 202, calling out, "Are you in there, girl? It's me, the one and original love of your life, Stringer MacKail."

A shy female voice on the far side answered, "The door's not locked, and for heaven's sake don't tell the whole world about us."

Stringer glanced both ways, dropped into a fighting crouch, and burst into the darkness, crabbing to one side to get a dark wall behind him as the dark figure on the bed gasped, "Oh, you're so impetuous!"

He covered her as he groped for a wall switch with his free hand. When the ceiling lights flashed on, she gasped again and hauled the sheet up over her entire. But not before he'd seen her naked cupcakes and swirling black hair. He blinked in surprise and asked, "What in thunder are *you* doing here?"

She giggled under the bed covers and replied, "Who were you expecting, the Queen of Sheba, you horny thing?"

As he suddenly grasped the full meaning of the grotesque telephone conversation he'd thought he'd been having with Pat Morrison Stringer laughed like hell, stepped out in the hall, and called out, "Forget it, gents. It was all a dumb mistake on my part and suffice it to say I don't seem to be in any danger after all."

Then he stepped back inside, locked the door, and switched off the lights. But once he was in bed with Rimfire Rowena he saw he might have spoken too soon. For she proceeded to endanger his health, if not his life, by screwing him beyond all common sense.

CHAPTER NINE

Later on, as they shared a smoke with the covers kicked off their sweat-slicked naked bodies, Rimfire Rowena insisted on telling him yet again how she'd never acted so wicked with just any man. He was too polite to point out that no woman could have ever learned to move so good, in some of the damnedest positions, without at least a little practice. It wouldn't have been fair to ask such questions about a lady's past, since he'd been as naughty with two other gals —make that three, now—since arriving in Wyoming just a few nights back.

"It was mean of you to accuse me of flirting with that colored man," she said, frowning real pretty. "I'll have you know I don't have anything going on with anyone connected with the Frontier Days. Couldn't you tell, just now, how frustrated I've been of late?"

He snuggled her closer with his free arm and assured her that made two of them. She dimpled, kissed his bare chest, and told him, "I know. I could tell when you talked to me on the telephone that you was out of your mind with hunger for my flesh. I was hoping you'd get around to some slap and tickle sooner or later, of course. But I must confess I never had a gent come out and just ask for it afore. Not any gent I wanted to do it with, least ways. Do you talk so direct and dirty to other women or did you want me extra special?"

He chuckled fondly and said, "I'm sorry I spoke to you so shocking before. I thought . . . I mean, I thought there was no sense beating about the bush with such a pretty little thing, seeing the rodeo's half over and you could have left town before we got past flowers, books, and candy."

She began to stroke his limp shaft, skillfully, as she said, "I know. I cussed myself good later for turning down your offer to buy me an ice cream soda. What do you suppose makes us gals so contrary when we see a nice-looking gent wants us? Why do we feel honor-bound to act so snippy, even when we want a man so bad we can taste it?"

He said, "Not being a woman, I've never worried about that too much. A man has to just accept the facts of nature as he finds 'em. Maybe if we men were stuck with giving our all to critters bigger, stronger, and more take-charge than us, we'd suffer some mixed emotions as well." Then he laughed and added, "Speaking of taking charge, though, don't I have anything to say about what you're doing to my poor thing right now?"

She gripped more firmly as she felt it responding to her playfulness and told him, "You don't have to do anything if it refuses to get hard again."

He reached out to snuff their smoke as he chuckled and told her, "You know damned well it's almost hard enough already."

She chuckled back, rolled atop him, and said, "Why, so it is," as she lowered herself to accept all he had to offer in a manner that made it rise to the occasion indeed. He was content to let her do all the work for now. He'd had a rough day after similar abuse from a less natural brunette the night before, and even if he hadn't, he couldn't have moved in Rimfire Rowena any faster, or better, than she was moving for him. But as he enjoyed the contrast between her smaller, more muscular torso and the softer more Junoesque charms of the gal called Cherokee, he was reminded of the fibs he'd told the law about the female situation in Iron Mountain. So he asked the one he was with, tonight, "Could I have your disinterested opinion on a moral dilemma that's been gawning at me, honey?"

She stopped and frowned down at him in the dim light to ask, "Are you worried about how moral we're acting, *now?* Can't you wait, damnit, until the cold gray dawn to ask if I still respect you?"

He said, "I'm not worried about being immoral with you. You've been doing fine. I've been thinking about another gal who . . ."

"While you're all the way inside of me, you son of a bitch?" she cut in, rolling off him to hit the mattress on her side with her back to him, cussing under her breath.

He patted her bare rump soothingly and explained, "I wasn't talking about making love to another gal, damnit. I was just wondering how far a man should go in lying for a friend. Turn over again, doll face. We can talk about it later, after we finish what we were just doing so nice."

She resisted. A gal who made her living aboard a show horse knew how to resist good. "That other gal must have been the bee's knees if you could even think of her, platonical, whilst I was making bare-ass love to you, you brute!"

"I'm sorry my mind drifted to dispolite," he said, stroking her thigh. "I hope you'll recall you had my undivided attention the first three times I was coming in you. Let me get on top and I'm sure I won't be able to think of anyone but you for a spell."

She sniffed and said, "I'm not much in the mood right now. Who was this durned old bawd you lie so much in favor of?"

"Well," he drawled, "since you ask, she wasn't exactly a bawd. She was a gal who warned me about a hired gun and likely saved my life."

"Before or after you'd screwed her?"

Stringer sighed and said, "She never warned me as a lover. I can't say for sure whether she was behaving in a Christian way or if she didn't want a shoot-out attracting the attention of the law to her surroundings. Either way, her warning gave me the edge I needed, and it was still close."

Interested, now, despite herself, Rimfire Rowena rolled over to ask, "Where does the lying come in, then?"

"Later," he said. "After she'd put me in her debt, I ran into some lawmen who may have been looking for her. I gave them a bum steer. I felt it was only my duty to a lady I owed my life to."

The lady in bed with him at the moment said, "I'll bet you owed her more than your life, you sex maniac. But what's the big deal about covering up for a gal you owed? It's a free country and you're not the law."

"I know. I'm not an outlaw, either, and if that gal is really who I suspect she could be, she and her friends were wanted serious. Ever since it happened, I've been chawing on whether I was right to pay back a debt of honor or wrong to aid and abet the Wild Bunch. For they're mighty wild as well as being a bunch, and if some innocent party was to get hurt because I failed to peach on a possible member of the gang..."

"Was she an outright bandit or just a gun moll?" Rimfire Rowena cut in.

"I'd say you could leave the gun off the moll in describing her. She may not even be the gal the law would like to question. But if she is, she's the sweetheart of a much more dangerous person," he explained.

Rimfire Rowena propped herself up on one elbow to shake her head clearer. Then she decided, "If you knew for certain she was someone really bad, it would have been your duty as a worthy citizen to turn her in. If you thought she was harmless, save for the company she keeps, I'd say you done right. Did she screw as good as me?"

Stringer laughed, shoved Rimfire Rowena on her back, and mounted her without answering. She protested that she didn't want to go sloppy seconds to any infernal outlaw gal. But after she found her hips responding to his manly thrusts she relented enough to grin up at him and say, "Well, if you've had that fool thing in anyone else for at least a month, you're just too ferocious to argue with. I'm sorry I called that poor outlaw gal a bawd. You have a mighty convincing way of proving your innocence and... Oh, Jeeee-zuss! Is this really the fourth... Don't stop! For I see it is and I want it to last forever!"

It couldn't, of course. So as they slowly drifted back down from heaven into each other's arms, Rimfire Rowena crooned, "Oh, Lord, that was lovely. I wish I wasn't leaving tomorrow, don't you?"

He kissed her throbbing throat and answered, "I didn't know you were. Don't the Frontier Days have a few days to go?"

She said, "Just the stock show and some more parades and stuff. The last rodeo events wind down tomorrow afternoon. They would've earlier this evening if it hadn't been for that sudden summer storm. They want me to ride in the opening warm-up, trick riding and shooting. They say I don't have to stay until the final awards. I'm paid flat for my act. So as soon as it's over I'm free to go."

He moved teasingly still in her and asked, "Don't you want to stick around and watch the rest of the show? I might buy you that ice cream soda afterwards."

She sighed. "Don't tempt me. It's good to hear you don't have no other gal here in Cheyenne. But honest injun, I have another rodeo to make in my slow-poke gypsy cart, and summer is the only time we can make money in my business, which is not the same business you've been moving in and out of me all night. So do you mean to give me the business again, or would you rather we saved some for morning? Once we have to get out of this bed, we won't be able to do it no more, unless you'd like to ride to Fort Collins with me—nice and slow."

Stringer sighed, rolled off her, and said he'd study on it, even though he had no reason to go that far south when he worked for a paper to the west. She snuggled closer and said, "I know. But at least we had tonight. I was so afraid you already had a gal here in Cheyenne. It must be the first time you was ever here, right?"

"I've passed through a time or more before," he said, "but the only lady I know here seems to have another lover. By the way, is anyone named Martin connected with the show tomorrow? The reason I ask is that while I know nobody named Martin will be riding, there could be, for all I know, a promoter, judge or whatever by that name."

She thought before she said, "There ain't. I'd have recalled the name because I had a... friend named Martin down in Texas one time. Why do you ask?"

He shrugged and said, "Long shot. Even if that other lady's boyfriend was named Martin, he wouldn't work as the right one. That gunslick I told you about, up at Iron

Mountain, had on a red silk rodeo shirt. But I can't see why the man who hired him would be interested in such matters."

She yawned. "Why did he want you so dead, then?"

Stringer yawned himself, and said, "Other matters, I reckon. I got sidetracked from the Frontier Days by what might have been a news scoop—if I'd just been able to find out a damned thing. I hope the mysterious Mister Martin knows by now how dumb I am. For I do mean to cover that rodeo tomorrow, and to do so I'll have to be sitting close in, with my fool back open to that whole considerable crowd in the stands. If even one of them is out to get me at this late date...Oh, hell," he murmured, snuggling in close to her and feeling the warmth of her body. "I can worry about it in the morning."

He did worry, in fact—all the way out to the fair grounds. But as long as Tom Horn refused to put all the cards on the table, there was just no way to tell his feature editor he had more important fish to fry. Since Rimfire Rowena had slipped away discreetly from the hotel ahead of him, Stringer had to walk all the way alone. With the road to the rodeo crowded with folks on foot, or in horse-drawn or horseless vehicles, walking backwards the whole way would have looked plain silly and still left his back exposed to more than he liked to think about. He spotted a Baker Electric passing, with a male and female outline facing one another through the sun-glared glass. If either belonged to Pat Morrison, she didn't see fit to stop and offer him a lift.

He saw the same vehicle later, parked outside the gate to the grand stands. He shrugged, got in line, and flashed his press pass at the vapidly pretty young gal taking tickets from most everyone else.

Once inside, Stringer strode at ground level between the rails protecting the crowd and the ever higher tiers of seats that were already starting to fill up. A little kid broke loose from his mom and charged Stringer's way waving a cotton candy cone like a Sioux on the warpath. Stringer blocked the little bastard, who counted coup on his jeans with sticky spun sugar, and hung on until his flustered and not-bad-looking mom could catch up and grab him by one ear, saying, "Thank you, sir. I don't know what's gotten into him today."

Stringer didn't see fit to offer an opinion of her tiny terror. The poor gal had enough on her plate. He told her boys would be boys, ticked his hat brim at her, and moved on.

A familiar voice called his name. He looked up to see Bat Masterson waving at him from the judging box. His fellow newsman yelled, "Climb up here, old son. The view is grand and there's plenty of room."

Stringer didn't see any steps on his side. But he found it easy enough to climb up hand over hand without tearing any of the red, white, and blue bunting draped over the sides.

He wasn't so sure he wanted to be there once he got there and saw who else was sharing the box with the easy-going panel of six judges. Pat Morrison was seated on a folding chair on the far side, with a sporty-looking young gent in a checked suit and derby. Pat was wearing a straw boater and a nifty outfit of rose velveteen. She looked as if butter wouldn't melt in her mouth as she glanced his way, nodded, and went back to jawing with the dude she'd come with.

As Stringer took a seat next to Bat Masterson, Judge Kenton, in front of them, turned in his seat, blinked at

Stringer, and said, "Well, this is a pleasant surprise. I thought you'd be up at Iron Mountain today, son."

"I almost was, your honor," Stringer replied. "I fear there's just nothing any of us can do for poor Tom Horn, though. I talked to him last night again. He keeps saying he has an alibi. But he refuses to say where he was and with whom at the time that kid was killed. So it's just his word against the arresting officer and I'd have likely had to go with the law against a known outlaw had I been on that jury."

Judge Kenton sighed and said, "I told you I'd read the transcripts and I'm glad I wasn't the presiding judge. I fear I'd have had to try him the same way. Joe LeFors, for all his faults, did put Horn behind that rocky outcrop, and since everybody had to be some-damned-where that fateful morning, it was up to Tom Horn to say where else he might have been. Calling the law a liar doesn't help much when a man insists he just can't recall where else he might have been at the time."

The older man shrugged in resignation and said, "At least the judging I have to do today won't involve half as much disputed testimony. Would you like to take part in our judging, seeing you must know more about the subject than any of us old city folk?"

Stringer shook his head and said, "No thanks, your honor. Some of the entrants are friends of mine and some could almost be called enemies—if they had more nerve. By the way, do you want those papers appointing me a sort of special whatever?"

Judge Kenton thought, shook his head, and said, "No, you may get lucky between now and the time you leave Cheyenne. They pack no authority anywhere else. But should you spot the murderer of Willie Nickell in the crowd today, feel free to arrest the son of a bitch."

Stringer cast a thoughtful look over his shoulder at all the faces way the hell up and back that had the drop on him. Suddenly Judge Kenton's words registered. "I didn't know your writ gave me arrest powers. What about other crooks I notice?"

The older man laughed and said, "Be my guest. I never appointed you a special investigator just to play patty-cakes with criminals... Oh," he added, suddenly turning away, "I see the show is about to begin."

Bat Masterson leaned over Stringer's way and asked what *that* had been all about. Stringer frowned. "Wild goose chase," he said. "I told you before about Tom Horn, remember?"

"I do," Masterson said, "and if you'll recall, I told you you were wasting your time. I'm still waiting to hear about that death trap at the hotel last night."

Stringer grinned sheepishly and said, "I got laid. Where's old Charlie Siringo now, by the way? I owe you both an apology for getting spooked over nothing."

"Charlie left for the South Pass County this morning. Something about the Wild Bunch. He ain't expecting any apology. You done right to get spooked. All of us old-timers have been spooked and acted accordingly in our time. That's how we got to be old-timers. They say James Butler Hickock was playing cards with his back to a whole saloon full of drunken strangers when he drew aces and eights. That wasn't being brave. That was being just plain stupid."

Before he could elaborate further a stocky newcomer in a too-big Stetson and too-loud lavender suit trimmed with white braid nudged Masterson and asked, "Do you mind?" So both Masterson and Stringer moved their seats to make room for his big purple rump. He sat down as if he owned the whole box and announced, "I am knowed as T.S.

Powers. Texas born and weaned, of course. But now I owns the Bar TS. You've heard of it, of course?"

Masterson said dryly, "I know what a bar looks like. What do the letters stand for—tough shit?"

Powers laughed and said, "You sure are a cute little rascal. What do they call you, Mud?"

Masterson said, "You got the initial right. The name is Masterson. William Bartholomew Masterson."

Powers replied, "Do tell? There used to be a Masterson down in Dodge. Some say he was sheriff and others say he was just a deputy. They called him Bat Masterson. Would you by any chance be related to him?"

Bat Masterson said, "No. I'm *him*. If you're through bragging, I'd like to watch the show now."

The cattle baron must have been. He went sort of dormant while a mess of white men dressed as Indians and at least a few real Indians dressed as cowboys paraded around waving the national and state colors to the sound of a brass band across the arena. It was hard to tell exactly what music they thought they were playing since it echoed back and forth between the tiers of seats. The cheaper ones way back against the skyline were so high above the ground that Stringer hoped that young mother and her pesky brat were seated further down the slope. A fall from that back row could prove something more fatal than any bucking critter could evoke.

As the cowboys, cowgirls, and Indians filed out of sight a mess of young gals charged in aboard trick ponies and proceeded to ride around the arena silly as hell. It was pretty to watch, though. Their shiny silk riding outfits left little at this range to a man's imagination. So it was interesting to consider how any gal who could contort her shape like that at full gallop would move in a more romantic setting. They jumped on and off, rode backwards and upside down, and when one fool gal actually fell off, the crowd gave her a splendid hand as she limped over to the rails, head down and rubbing her silk-clad rump.

Then the clowns, dressed more like hobo drunks, set up pipe racks with balloons, clay pipes, and Christmas tree balls swinging on strings of various lengths. Stringer nudged Bat and said, "I'll bet this is where Rimfire Rowena makes her entance."

She did indeed, standing straight up with her soft-soled boots planted on the bobbing rump of her painted pony, going lickety-split with her leather skirt flapping in the breeze, her black hair streaming under her wide sombrero, and a long-barreled pistol in each hand.

She had that pony really trained. It ran around in the same big circle as if it thought it belonged on a merry-go-round. But just the same, it took a lot of skill to ride like that, and even more to pop free-hand with each pistol in turn and never miss.

The crowd went wild as Rimfire Rowena demolished target after target until half of them were gone. Then she spun like a ballet dancer to drop into her saddle, riding backwards as she holstered both pistols and got out a saddle carbine. Those in the crowd who knew how hard it was applauded as she commenced to pick off her targets after she'd passed them instead of the more spectacular but easier way. But T.S. Powers grumbled, "I'll bet she's got pepper-shot in that gun."

Stringer asked mildly, "Do you reckon you could shoot like that with a fire hose?"

Bat Masterson nudged him and murmured, "The man's entitled to his opinion, kid." So Stringer shut up, knowing Masterson had some reason for being so nice to such an idiot.

It wasn't easy. As Rimfire Rowena finished off the last

target and circled the ring standing up again with her arms thrown wide and her head thrown back, as if she was leaning into the roar of the crowd, the big mouth laughed lewdly and said, "Well, nobody can say she don't have a nice little set of tits. How'd you boys like to get some of that, eh?"

"Be careful," Stringer countered as flat as he could without losing his temper, "I hear her current boyfriend packs a gun."

So the cattle baron said, "Just funning. She'd likely be all whipcord and whalebone anyway. I likes my women soft and snugglesome."

They had to sit through some trick rope spinning next. At least they could all agree that whilst one of the rope spinners looked a little swishy, none of them felt like going to bed with *him*.

Then it got sort of quiet. They were close enough to hear the announcer, but it was doubtful the folk in the higher seats did. They all acted surprised when the first calf came out of the chutes with a roper chasing after it at a dead run. The first roper missed and reined to a stop, shaking his head morosely as he hauled his rope back in. Nobody booed and some, including Stringer, gave him a polite hand. It was a western crowd. So more than one of them knew how easy it was to miss.

The next roper caught his calf and had it hog-tied in just under a minute. Bat Masterson thought that was pretty good. But Stringer said, "He's out of the money with that time unless nobody else shows up intent on serious roping."

Some were and some weren't. Two other riders missed and one busted his rope. As the crowd applauded the last calf roper Judge Kenton turned around in his seat to tell

Stringer, "I make it rider number eight for first place. How about you?"

Stringer nodded and said, "Yessir. He has the best time by a full second. His name's O'Hara and he hails from Helena."

Judge Kenton asked, "Do you know him, then?"

Stringer fanned the notebook in his hand as he answered, "I do now. I found the names and numbers posted together when I took 'em down last night. I make Parker number twelve, and Hall, number ten, for second and third place."

Judge Kenton said, "I had them tied. But since your eyes may be younger and sharper than mine, I'll go along with you on that." Then he turned back to pow-wow with the other old gents. He seemed to have the Indian sign on his fellow townees. So now Stringer was painfully aware he had to pay attention, lest he screw some deserving rider with a careless opinion. Just thinking about it made him itch between the shoulder blades. But since he had no eyes in the back of his head—so what the hell.

They cleared the tanbark to get ready for the next event. Apparently, the prissy dude with Pat Morrison must have decided that was a good chance to buy her some cotton candy or maybe take a leak. He'd no sooner left the box when Pat came over, bent her lips close to Stringer's frozen face, and asked, "Did you telephone me last night, dear?"

He asked, "How come you thought it was me?"

"I didn't," she replied, "until just now. I thought you'd still be up at Iron Mountain."

He couldn't resist casting a sardonic glance at her escort's empty chair as he said, "I don't see what difference it makes."

She smiled, a bit too brightly, and said, "Good heavens, he's simply another client. Is that why you didn't even speak to me before? You're not jealous of another *client*, are you?"

He smiled up at her thinly and said, "I might have been, had you and me exchanged any promises along them lines, Pat. Would you like to pin a name on your ... ah ... client? I can assure you my reasons for asking are platonic."

She looked confused and said, "His name is Martin Dobbs and he's in the insurance business, if you must know. Why do you ask?"

"I'm paid to ask questions," Stringer said flatly. "You'd best get back to your seat now. The next event is fixing to start."

She asked, "Will you call me later?"

"Sure," he said looking stone-faced, "if I need a lawyer." She left, looking a mite hurt.

Bat Masterson leaned over to Stringer. "What was that all about?"

"Likely nothing," Stringer frowned. "The Mister Martin that's been giving me so much trouble seems to have a nasty sense of humor. He'd hardly send a persuader to threaten a gal if he already had a nicer notion. Gals don't keep secrets worth a hang when you have 'em in a really friendly mood."

Masterson shook his head and said, "I don't know how you do it, kid. I've never considered myself the hunchback of Notre Dame. But I generally have to be in a town at least a week before I'm juggling two gals at once."

Stringer knew his pal would think he was bragging if he said he'd had *three* since arriving in Cheyenne. Instead, he just said, "Let's watch the show."

The more serious steer busting came after the calf roping. He knew harder work deserved bigger prizes and leaned forward to ask Judge Kenton what kind of money they were talking about.

When the judge mentioned a figure lower than Stringer had expected, he leaned back and told Bat, "I'm glad I gave up working cows. Everything but top hand wages has gone up since the glory days of the beef boom."

Masterson nodded and said, "It always was a trade for total idiots. That's likely why we call 'em cow *boys*. No grown man with a lick of sense would work that hard and take as many chances for forty dollars a month."

"If he gets that much," Stringer pointed out, adding, "you're talking top hand wages. I reckon that's why a rider who sees a crack at three or four figures for a day's work is willing to work this hard and... Oh, oh, that was a bad fall."

He and many of the others rose from their seats for a better view as the clowns and some of the hands rail-birded closer ran out to do something about the steer roper who'd dropped his noose on too much beef and wound up going down pony and all. The pony appeared to be all right. It was already back up, with a hand chasing it. Its rider lay sprawled like a rag doll on the tanbark. It could take a lot out of a rider to have his mount roll over him like that.

But as they got the hurt rider aboard a litter, a familiar figure dressed all in brown rose clear, turned to the crowd, and gave the thumbs-up sign. As everyone else heaved a mighty sigh and began to clap in unison the cattle baron seated near them grumbled, "What's that nigger in the brown outfit doing here?"

Stringer answered, "He's half Choctaw and all cowhand. I'd say he was here for some prize money."

T.S. Powers snorted in disgust and said, "That'll be the day. The Good Lord never meant to put no nigger on a horse. It was Abe Lincoln's fool notion. I wouldn't hire a nigger to dig post holes. They may know picking cotton, but the skills of a cowhand are beyond their small brains."

Bat Masterson said, "Oh, I don't know. My pard here just said that boy was part Indian. What kind of a wager did you have in mind, T.S.?"

The beefy cattle baron frowned at Masterson and said, "I don't recall making any wager on anything."

Masterson laughed lightly. "Oh, I didn't know you was all talk. I thought you were a sport. Forget it."

Old T.S. didn't want to. He blustered, "I guess I'm as good a sport as anyone else I see around here. But what are we betting on, damnit?"

Masterson said, "That colored boy. You say he doesn't belong in a rodeo. My young pard here says he's a tolerable cowhand. I've got a hundred dollars I was saving for more disgusting vices, but if you'd like to cover it, it might make this show more interesting for both of us."

Powers frowned suspiciously and asked, "What event is that nigger signed in for?"

Masterson replied, "Don't ask me. I just now laid eyes on the boy. It can't be roping since he'd already be over in the chutes by now if it was. I reckon it has to be something else, don't you?"

Powers hesitated, then asked, "Even money?"

"You're a hard man to do business with," Masterson replied. "We both know that for every winner there has to be a lot more losers. But all right, put your money where your mouth is, and old Stringer can hold the purse for us."

The bet was soon arranged, but not before the first longhorn charged out of the chutes with a rider flanking it to either side. Neither were swinging ropes. The rider to the steer's left dove headfirst out of his saddle to grab the brute's horns and start wrestling with it. T.S. Powers gasped and demanded, "What in the name of God's Green Pastures does that fool think he's doing to that longhorn?"

So Masterson explained, "They call it bulldogging. It's

a sort of new way to bust a steer. You got to remember this is the dawn of the twentieth century, pard."

The bulldogger got a round of applause as he finally managed to put the bigger brute on the ground, horn tips to the tanbark. Stringer said, "That time's going to cost old Richardson, number twenty-six from Arizona Territory. Takes a bigger man to throw that much beef about."

T.S. Powers opined it was the dumbest way to down a cow that he'd ever seen. Then chute number three popped open and the black rider they'd been arguing about chased his longhorn a few paces, dropped on its wicked horns, and had them both planted in the tanbark in less than five seconds. As Bill Pickett leaped to his feet again, arms triumphantly wide, the crowd tried to knock him back down with a thunderous applause. As the clapping died down, Powers said, "The event ain't over. I might have knowed a nigger would grab a cow dirty."

Bat Masterson said, "Cheer up. All the other riders may be pale faces, and for all we know, one or more could beat that time."

But nobody else came anywhere close to Pickett's time, and when the event was over, Judge Kenton turned again to say, "I make it numbers seventeen, thirty-two and eight. You?"

Stringer said, "Same way, your honor. O'Hara figures to go home with some mighty drinking money indeed if he places in any more events after winning that one."

Then he handed Masterson the two hundred dollars and murmured low, "I don't suppose you knew old Bill Pickett invented bulldogging in the Year of Our Lord 1901, eh?"

As Masterson put the money away he looked innocent and said, "Hell, kid, a famous sportswriter like me is supposed to know such things. But it's true I never saw Bill Pickett do it before. So it was a fair wager at even money."

T.S. Powers stood up, red faced, and announced, "If you wasn't so famous in other ways, Mister Masterson, I might have more to say about how you just slickered me." And then he grumped his way out of the box.

"I don't know, Bat," Stringer said, watching that fat purple suit waddle away. "You made that old boy sort of mad at you and he could have all sorts of gents on his payroll."

Masterson shrugged and said, "That's why I never took him for real money. Nobody's about to go up against my rep for less than a thousand. Well, five hundred, anyways."

Stringer said, "I wish I knew what my life was worth, or if anyone was still putting up the money."

Masterson said, "You're likely in the clear now. You don't know anything about Tom Horn that I don't know, and nobody seems to be after me."

Stringer had some reservations about that. For one thing he knew Tom Horn had some hare-brained escape plans. Unless his old pards were dumb as he was, they could have smuggled him that gun he didn't know how to use as a good way to shut him up forever. They wouldn't want a reporter Horn was in the habit of confiding in to spill that bean. On the other hand, they'd tried to stop him long before anyone had managed to get that Luger in to old Tom. He turned to Masterson and said, "Bat, I was just thinking. What if all the trouble I've been having has nothing at all to do with Tom Horn or that Nickell boy?"

Masterson frowned. "Didn't they send a hired gun to kill you up at Iron Mountain, where it all began?"

"Yeah," Stringer said, "and some local toughs gave me a hard time, too. But I'm pretty sure they were acting on their own in the interest of xenophobia. The folk up there just seem to want to forget the case and leave things the way they are. My troubles with serious gunslicks started here in Cheyenne. Billy Gower *followed* me to Iron Mountain after I crawfished his pard, Friendly Frank, here in town. I ran that one out of this town, not Iron Mountain, last night. What if, all this time, they've been trying to keep me from reporting something they're up to right here in Cheyenne?"

Masterson pursed his lips and asked, "Aside from Tom Horn, you mean? They'd be dumb as hell if that was their game. For while Lord only knows what could be going on behind closed shutters in a town this size, you only came to cover this fool rodeo, right?"

"Yes," Stringer nodded, "and if they'd just left me alone I wouldn't have missed any of it."

"You didn't miss much," Masterson said. "All the good stuff is taking place about now. The mastermind behind all your woes can't be worried about you writing a feature on the Frontier Days. For that's what I'm doing, and there's dozens of other newspapermen here today to do the same thing, even if they don't have such good seats. Me and Charlie Siringo had a drink with Richard Harding Davis after we left you last night. He said he'd heard Jack London might show up as well."

Stringer shook his head and said, "I ran into London over in the Yellowstone Park a short spell back. He's covering Teddy Roosevelt's western tour, so about now they're seeing the troops off to the Philippines. Davis is a fair reporter, though."

Masterson said, "There you go. Even if you was dead, these Frontier Days would still get written up fairly accurate. Like I said, it has to be something sneakier than a wide-open rodeo with half the world in the stands. Are you sure you didn't stumble into a back room uninvited or ask some dumb question that could be taken wrong, kid?"

"I'm always asking dumb questions," Stringer answered. Then he shot a side-glance across the box, to where the checkered and derbied dude called Martin had rejoined Pat Morrison. He thought before he decided, "Naw, he don't look that jealous and my troubles started before I ever knew his new girl friend. If he's a well-known local businessman, it's easy enough to see why someone grabbed his name out of thin air. Crooks hardly ever use their real name, even with other crooks."

Judge Kenton turned around to ask, "Who do you like in the bull riding, son?"

Stringer had to admit, "I fear I just wasn't paying attention, your honor. You're an official contest judge, and so far, you've been calling 'em as good as I could."

Judge Kenton said, "All right. Young O'Hara winds up in the money again. What's the matter, son? You look sort of green around the gills."

"I got a lot on my mind, sir," Stringer replied, so the judge turned around to see who'd win the bare-back bronc event.

Stringer nudged Masterson and said, "Try to keep tabs on first, place and show for me, will you, Bat? I got to stretch my legs."

"Sure," Masterson said, "and piss once for me while you're at it," as Stringer swung a long leg over the edge of the box. He didn't say that wasn't where he was going. He wasn't sure where he was going just yet.

CHAPTER TEN

By the time Stringer had talked to enough show riders to get things straight in his head the show was over a spell and most everyone else had left. So Stringer was able to walk straight across the tanbark toward the judges' box with Rimfire Rowena and a half-dozen tougher-looking riders in tow, including old Slash. When they got to the box, Stringer saw Bat Masterson, Pat Morrison, and her insurance slicker had already left, along with a few officials. That left plenty of room for Stringer and his friends as they climbed into the box, and luckily the officials and promoters Stringer really wanted to talk to were still there.

Judge Kenton smiled. "You missed some pretty good saddle bronc riding, son. Where have you been all this time?"

"Talking to these other folk, your honor. Now we'd like to talk about the money they have coming."

Judge Kenton pointed at a younger and harder-eyed gent in an undertaker's frock coat, who said, "I'm Wes Keller, the treasurer, and I can assure one and all that the prize money anyone has coming is safe and secure in my paywagon."

Stringer said, "We know. Big Bill Pickett and Swede Larson are guarding it, with their hardware strapped on. Nobody is about to even smell that money until we have a full accounting."

Stringer glanced at the other worried old gents and assured them, "None of you have anything to worry about. You were all being used as dupes, too."

He realized it had been a mistake to take his eyes off Keller when Rimfire Rowena drew and fired her target pistol. It was almost an insult to shoot a grown man with a .32 short. But when Rimfire Rowena fired she hit what she was aiming at. Her bitty slug went into Keller's right ear hole to wind up smack in the center of his brain. So he dropped like a felled ox with his more serious sidearm in hand but only half clear of its holster.

Stringer stared soberly down at the body on the planks between them and said, "Thanks." Then he saw that Judge Kenton had lit out and up, striding across the empty bleachers with amazing agility. Stringer lit out after him.

As he started to gain near the top he called out, "It's no use, your honor. By the powers invested in me by your court I just have to arrest you, on the charge of criminal fraud. But hell, with your sidekick dead you have an outside chance of beating us in court. So why don't you cut this foolishness?"

The old man didn't answer or even look back. He kept on going until, near the top, even he must have noticed there was no place higher to climb. He stopped with his feet planted wide on the very top seats and the guard rail waist high behind him. Stringer slowed his own pace but kept moving up as he called, "Give it up, your honor. I never did get the hang of algebra, but I can add simple figures tolerable. I knew I had you, Mister Martin, as soon as I matched the total prize money alongside all the entry fees. But we both know Lawyer Morrison is slick as well as sort of passionate. She might be able to add the figures up in a way a jury could find confusing. Nobody else around here seems half as good at simple addition as me."

The once distinguished-looking older man made funny croaking noises as he stared wildly about from his perch. He saw Rimfire Rowena coming across the seats at a more ladylike pace to the left of Stringer. The surly-faced Slash was coming faster to Stringer's right. Judge Kenton gave a strangled cry, and as Stringer bawled, "No! Don't try that!" the trapped official rolled over the guard rail and dropped out of sight.

Stringer turned to run down the seats a lot faster than he'd been climbing them, with Slash and Rimfire Rowena following his lead. By the time they made it outside via an exit gate at ground level, other rodeo riders had made it to where Judge Kenton lay sprawled on his back, staring up at the gloaming sky with a sort of relaxed little smile on his dead lips.

Stringer hunkered down to feel the old man's ribcage and make sure. Then he nodded and said, "Whether he intended suicide or figured on landing at a run from that high up, the results were the same. I wish he hadn't gotten so excited. When he wasn't being Mister Martin I sort of liked the old son of a bitch."

When Bat Masterson caught up later that evening at the Drover's Palace, Stringer remembered they'd agreed to share all coverage. So he herded Bat into the tap room and they toted a bottle of bourbon and a pitcher of beer to a corner table. Since Stringer was paying, Bat said he'd be proud to carry the shot glasses and beer schooners.

They sat down. Setting the glasses down, Masterson said, "I sent a mess of wires right after word reached me about that swan-dive out to the fair grounds. The promoters who put that rodeo together have been doing the same in other parts for some time now, and they seem no worse than most—and better than some—when it comes to crooking folk."

Stringer poured for both of them and said, "All but *one* of them. They hired a professional accountant to act as their money handler this spring as their shows got bigger and the bookkeeping got above their rustic heads. His name was Wes Keller, and the reason he was available was that he'd been fired, more than once, for letting his former employer's money sort of evaporate. The rodeo promoters didn't know this, of course. Keller was so slick at evaporating money that it was easier to just fire him, leaving him with no outright criminal record."

Stringer inhaled half the contents of his shot glass, washed it down with a slug of suds, and continued, "Keller's bookkeeping for the rodeo promoters was even slicker. He kept careful and honest track of all the ticket sales and concession fees. The boys putting on the shows got every red cent coming to them after expenses, and since he was careful and tight with expense vouchers, the gents he was working for were delighted with the profits he could show 'em in the honest books he kept on that subject."

Masterson frowned thoughtfully and said, "I thought you just said he was a crook."

Stringer nodded. "I said he was a slick one. Way too slick to crook the gents he worked with regular. He recorded the entry fees and prize money in another set of books. *Two* of 'em—one, the way they should have read, in the unlikely event his employers ever wanted to cast a passing glance over them. The figures he kept secretly in a bottom drawer—we just now went over 'em—they read a lot more sneaky. He recorded the entry fees just as they were collected. He was smart enough to see that riders following the rodeo circuit had a fair grasp on the going rates for attempting suicide on horseback. As we all know, all that money was supposed to be divided fair and awarded in total to the winners of each event."

Bat Masterson nodded in both grim and sudden understanding as he growled, "How much of the prize money was he skimming?"

"Better than half," Stringer said.

"Aw, come on, nobody could be *that* dumb," Masterson said.

Stringer insisted. "There was little reason for anyone to be all that smart. The promoters, being no more dishonest than anyone else who's ever paid a cowhand what the poor cuss is willing to work for, had no call to worry about the entry fees. They'd written that off as prize money and none of them were about to enter their own rodeo. Keller saw to it that they were getting their cut of every cotton candy cone. They had no need to distrust him. So they never did."

Masterson poured the next round as he pointed out, "The riders surely had a vested interest in their own money, didn't they?"

"They did," Stringer said, taking a big gulp of bourbon. "And you pointed out earlier that very few gents with a grasp of high finances ever take to the carefree riding and roping trade to begin with. Like I said, each entrant knew how much he'd personally put in the pot. He had no call to ask many others what they might or might not have paid, and if he had, he'd still have needed a pencil, paper, and more education than your average country boy to come up with the grand total. The entry fee depends on which event you want to enter. A man entering the saddle bronc event might not want to know what a sissy calf roper chipped in. We're talking a mighty big show with all sorts of riders from all over the country. So all each rider was sure of, or really cared about, was whether or not he finished in the money or how much he was out if he lost."

Masterson grimaced. "As a sportswriter of some experience, I have never been all that inspired by the athletic brain. But a fifty percent rake-off?"

"It was raw, but not that hard to get away with," Stringer explained, "considering the size of the show. Naturally the boys entering such a swamping rodeo expected bigger prizes than usual, and since there were so many entry fees to skim, Keller was able to set aside prizes big enough to be impressive even if they were hardly what the winners really had coming. He figured the winners would be pleased as punch to wind up with more money than what they could make in a year poking cows, while the disgruntled losers cold hardly give a damn. He was likely right. Only now the more honest showmen will be working things out more decent with the boys, who'll now all be moving on with what they really won, see?"

"Nope," Masterson said. "All you've explained, so far, is how come Wes Keller wound up with a bullet in his ear. Where do Tom Horn and Judge Kenton fit in?"

"Put Tom Horn on the back of the stove for now. First, Wes Keller had to recruit at least one local official who could easily turn crooked. To keep the big show looking halfways honest, the promoters made it their custom to ask local city officials to sit in with them as impartial judges."

"Kenton was a judge who could be bought," Masterson agreed. "I told you I'd been asking about him by wire. But I was there with you this afternoon and you said he was calling the shots about the way you would have." Then he reached under his frock coat, got out a rodeo program with pencil scrawls on its blank side, and added, "By the way, here's the numbers that won after you jumped out of the box and run off to ask questions."

Stringer put the coverage away with a nod of thanks and said, "The crooked treasurer didn't ask Kenton to judge any event the wrong way. Too many experts on the subject would have been sure to notice. It was also the custom for the judges, not the promoters themselves, to award the cash prizes, blue-ribbon bows, and such. Keller didn't want anyone to even hint that he and he alone was distributing the money entrusted to his care, see?"

"No." Masterson was feeling dense. "What about all those other pillars of the community? Was they supposed to be blind?"

"Yep. Once Judge Kenton agreed to head the judging panel, guess who got to select 'em?"

"Oh, I noticed he seemed to have the last word this afternoon. He picked easy-going members of the courthouse gang who'd go along with about anything he said, right?"

"Right. He made sure they were all townees, more honored than aware of what the hell they were doing at any rodeo. I doubt any of 'em knew the contest rules any better than a little crank I met out there who smeared my jeans with cotton candy. They had no idea how much money might have been collected as entry fees and no call to question the wisdom of the good old boy who'd asked them all to sit in with him. Had things gone as planned, Judge Kenton would have given each winner a sincere smile, a hearty handshake, and half the prize money he had coming."

Bat Masterson whistled softly. "Yep, that's so dirty it would almost have to work. Nobody halfway honest could think half that dirty. So what put you on to it, you dirty cuss?"

Stringer smiled thinly and said, "They did. Or maybe I should say it was someone's guilty conscience. You see, no offense, it was hardly likely you or any other average newsman covering the show knew as much as yours truly about the finer points of rodeo riding."

Masterson growled, "All right, so you've likely stepped in more cow shit than the rest of us in our time. But you just said a lot of old cowhands were there to observe any wrong moves."

Stringer nodded and said, "I was the one with a college education as well. Worse yet, from their point of view, last fall I wrote a feature on the big Denver show, and it's likely they'd read it. I didn't catch any crooks at that other show. But I did publish some pungent observations on the unfairness of asking a rider to pay for the privilege of risking his own neck. So when they discovered I was here to cover this show, they paid me the compliment of assuming I was here to turn in an exposé on them, and they had a good thing going that they just didn't want exposed. It was easy enough for a shady judge to look up shady characters. So they sent Friendly Frank to run me out of town, and when that didn't work, they asked an even meaner gunslick to shut me up before I had anything to say."

"What about Tom Horn?" asked Masterson.

"That comes later. I had no idea why someone had it in for me. Tom Horn contacted me on his own. After I'd heard his sad story I made the dumb but natural mistake of assuming someone wanted him hung so bad that they were willing to gun me to keep me from uncovering new evidence in his favor. I picked a lawyer at random and..."

"She was that good-looking gal who you didn't want to talk to this afternoon, right?" Masterson cut in.

Stringer nodded and said, "She was innocent of anything but a sort of friendly view on lawyer-client relationships. But I suspect Judge Kenton must have known she had that other client called Martin Dobbs."

Stringer sipped some more beer and went on. "When she brought me for help to a judge she had down as honest, old Kenton must have nigh shat in his pants. But he was a cool old cuss and then I, like a fool, told him what a fool I was. I don't know how he kept from busting out laughing when I told him I suspected the hired gun—which he'd sent after me—was involved some way with old Tom Horn. But, thinking fast, he offered me all the help I could ask for in hopes of freeing an innocent man."

"Do you think Tom Horn is innocent?" Masterson asked.

"Beats the shit out of me," Stringer said, downing another slug of bourbon. "It works as well both ways. He could be lying. Joe LeFors could be lying. The point is that Judge Kenton didn't give a shit either way. He'd sent old Friendly Frank to run me out of town and make me miss the rodeo and here I was offering to go! So he sent me off to Iron Mountain with his blessings, figuring I wouldn't get back until he and Wes Keller had divided the spoils of their crooked scheme."

Masterson nodded and said, "You sure acted foolish. But how come they still sent that rascal Billy Gower to pick a fight with you? Killing has gotten sort of serious lately, and they knew you couldn't do them no damage way the hell up north."

Stringer said, "It works both ways. With both masterminds dead we'll never know for sure. But either Gower had been sent after me already, and meant to collect no matter where he nailed my hide, or Judge Kenton figured that no matter which of us won, I'd be stuck up in Iron Mountain for a good spell, waiting on a coroner's jury to clear me."

Masterson chuckled. "It's a good thing Gower had all

that bounty money posted on him. The law liked to keep good deals to itself when I was working down at Dodge that time. Judge Kenton must have felt like shitting his pants some more when you showed up to cover the prize events after all."

Stringer smiled. "Judge Kenton took first place for calm and grace under pressure. They had no choice but to brazen it out and hope I was still too distracted by wild goose feathers to notice what was going on right under my nose."

"In fact," he added, giving a big sigh, "they almost got away with it. I was sitting there with so many things going through my fool head at once that I was barely paying attention to the rodeo. I knew Friendly Frank had likely fibbed to me about working for Mister Martin. Yet there was my lawyer-gal, sitting there with another client called Martin Dobbs. He was easy enough to dislike. But he just wouldn't work as the mastermind. Then it hit me that old Pat made a habit of taking clients to one sweet old judge she had an in with, and that even an insurance man needed a special invite to sit like a swell in the judging stand, so, hell, I wasn't *that* dumb."

Masterson nodded and said, "Nobody said you were. I reckon that had *I* any reason to start wondering about that judge I'd have only had to ask a few more questions to put the puzzle together. I've always known that a liar who needs to come up with a phony name in a hurry tends to grab the name of someone he may know casual, not bothering to study on just where he's heard it. I might not have been as quick to come up with their prize money swindle. But as they were so worried, any investigative reporter worth his snout would have rooted up the rest, once he'd scented buried scandal." He picked up the bourbon bottle for another pour, then asked, "Where might you be off to next, Stringer, now that we've both wound up with such a fine scoop?"

"Well, my feature will have to be wired in a mite ahead of the rest of me, Bat. The Cheyenne district attorney has asked for sworn depositions and the county coroner would like our views on just how one crook wound up with a bullet in his head and another wound up with a busted neck. So I don't see how Miss Rimfire Rowena or me would be leaving Cheyenne for at least a few more days."

"And nights," observed Bat Masterson as he raised his glass with a knowing grin and added, "I doubt you'll suffer all that much, even if that dumb old fart in the lavender suit did opine she seemed mostly whipcord and whalebone."

Stringer raised his own glass to reply, soberly, "You're right. He surely was a dumb old fart."

EPILOGUE

It was fun while it lasted, but neither Rimfire Rowena nor Stringer felt any call to remain in Cheyenne well into the fall, when the sad saga of Tom Horn was finally resolved.

So Stringer could only rely on the coverage of other reporters, who seemed to have had trouble agreeing on all of the details.

Whether Tom Horn's pals busted him out with that dynamite, as some would have it, or whether the plot was exposed and old Tom simply got the drop on his guards and vacated the premises more sedately, all agree he busted out and didn't get too far.

Cornered in a downtown alley a short distance from the Cheyenne Jail, the old Apache fighter forted up behind a horseless carriage he didn't know how to start, with a gun he didn't know how to use. For whether that German Luger had been smuggled in to him by pals who should have known better or, as some said, it'd been slipped to him by a corrupt guard who just didn't care, the no-longer-young gunfighter hadn't kept up with the times.

Years later the more adaptable Henry Starr would make the transition from old-style western outlaw to first of the modern gangsters by swapping his pony for a Model T Ford to hold up an Oklahoma bank in the summer of 1914.

But the barely literate Tom Horn was forced to surrender to his grinning enemies when he simply couldn't get his newfangled weapon to back his desperate ploy.

So on a cold November morning the tough but not-too-bright Tom Horn died game on the up-to-date hydraulic gallows Wyoming was so proud of. All who witnessed the execution agreed that the wonders of modern science left much to be desired.

Tom Horn stood in hooded silence on the trap as they all got to listen to the protracted gurgle of water in the toilet-tank mechanism for quite a spell. Then, at last, it was over.

Stringer never believed, as some would have it, that Tom Horn had been hanged with that handsome show rope they'd allowed him to braid in his cell as he was sweating out his date with a much stouter, and uglier, length of hangman's hemp.

As to whether Tom Horn deserved to die for the murder of young Willie Nickell, or whether—as many still feel—he was framed for local political reasons, there are still places in the cow country of Wyoming where it's just not wise to say you know for certain, either way.

MEET STRINGER MacKAIL
NEWSMAN, GUNMAN, LADIES' MAN.

LOU CAMERON'S
STRINGER

*"STRINGER's the hardest ridin',
hardest fightin' and hardest lovin' hombre
I've had the pleasure of encountering
in quite a while."*
—Tabor Evans, author of the LONGARM series

It's the dawn of the twentieth century
and the Old West is drawing to a close. But for
Stringer MacKail, the shooting's just begun.

_0-441-79064-X	STRINGER	$2.75
_0-441-79022-4	STRINGER ON DEAD MAN'S RANGE #2	$2.75
_0-441-79074-7	STRINGER ON THE ASSASSINS' TRAIL #3	$2.75
_0-441-79078-X	STRINGER AND THE HANGMAN'S RODEO #4	$2.75
_0-55773-010-5	STRINGER AND THE WILD BUNCH #5	$2.75

Please send the titles I've checked above. Mail orders to:
BERKLEY PUBLISHING GROUP
390 Murray Hill Pkwy., Dept. B
East Rutherford, NJ 07073

NAME_____
ADDRESS_____
CITY_____
STATE_____ZIP_____

Please allow 6 weeks for delivery.
Prices are subject to change without notice.

POSTAGE & HANDLING:
$1.00 for one book, $.25 for each
additional. Do not exceed $3.50.

BOOK TOTAL	$_____
SHIPPING & HANDLING	$_____
APPLICABLE SALES TAX (CA, NJ, NY, PA)	$_____
TOTAL AMOUNT DUE	$_____
PAYABLE IN US FUNDS. (No cash orders accepted.)	

LONGARM

Explore the exciting Old West with one of the men who made it wild!

__0-515-08965-6	LONGARM #1	$2.75
__0-515-08966-4	LONGARM ON THE BORDER #2	$2.75
__0-515-08967-2	LONGARM AND THE AVENGING ANGELS #3	$2.75
__0-515-08968-0	LONGARM AND THE WENDIGO #4	$2.75
__0-515-08969-9	LONGARM IN THE INDIAN NATION #5	$2.75
__0-515-08970-2	LONGARM AND THE LOGGERS #6	$2.75
__0-515-08971-0	LONGARM AND THE HIGHGRADERS #7	$2.75
__0-515-08972-9	LONGARM AND THE NESTERS #8	$2.75
__0-515-07414-4	LONGARM IN THE BIG THICKET #48	$2.50
__0-515-07854-9	LONGARM IN THE BIG BEND #50	$2.50
__0-515-07722-4	LONGARM ON THE GREAT DIVIDE #52	$2.50
__0-515-09287-8	LONGARM AND THE FRONTIER DUCHESS #81	$2.75
__0-515-09288-6	LONGARM AND THE TENDERFOOT #83	$2.75
__0-515-09289-4	LONGARM AND THE STAGECOACH BANDITS #84	$2.75
__0-515-09290-8	LONGARM IN THE HARD ROCK COUNTRY #86	$2.75
__0-515-09291-6	LONGARM IN THE TEXAS PANHANDLE #87	$2.75

Please send the titles I've checked above. Mail orders to:

BERKLEY PUBLISHING GROUP
390 Murray Hill Pkwy., Dept. B
East Rutherford, NJ 07073

NAME_____

ADDRESS_____

CITY_____

STATE_____ZIP_____

Please allow 6 weeks for delivery.
Prices are subject to change without notice.

POSTAGE & HANDLING:
$1.00 for one book, $.25 for each additional. Do not exceed $3.50.

BOOK TOTAL	$_____
SHIPPING & HANDLING	$_____
APPLICABLE SALES TAX (CA, NJ, NY, PA)	$_____
TOTAL AMOUNT DUE PAYABLE IN US FUNDS. (No cash orders accepted.)	$_____

LONGARM

Explore the exciting Old West with one of the men who made it wild!

__0-515-08607-X	LONGARM AND THE GREAT CATTLE KILL #91	$2.50
__0-515-08675-4	LONGARM ON THE SIWASH TRAIL #93	$2.75
__0-515-08754-8	LONGARM AND THE ESCAPE ARTIST #95	$2.75
__0-515-08796-3	LONGARM AND THE BONE SKINNERS #96	$2.75
__0-515-08838-2	LONGARM AND THE MEXICAN LINE-UP #97	$2.75
__0-515-08883-8	LONGARM AND THE TRAIL DRIVE SHAM #98	$2.75
__0-515-08907-9	LONGARM AND THE DESERT SPIRITS #99	$2.75
__0-515-08934-6	LONGARM ON DEATH MOUNTAIN #100	$2.75
__0-515-08959-1	LONGARM AND THE COTTONWOOD CURSE #101	$2.75
__0-515-09007-7	LONGARM AND THE DESPERATE MANHUNT #102	$2.75
__0-515-09056-5	LONGARM AND THE ROCKY MOUNTAIN CHASE #103	$2.75
__0-515-09113-8	LONGARM ON THE OVERLAND TRAIL #104	$2.75
__0-515-09169-3	LONGARM AND THE BIG POSSE #105	$2.75
__0-515-09215-0	LONGARM ON DEADMAN'S TRAIL #106	$2.75
__0-515-09256-8	LONGARM IN THE BIGHORN BASIN #107	$2.75
__0-515-09325-4	LONGARM AND THE BLOOD HARVEST #108	$2.75
__0-515-09378-5	LONGARM AND THE BLOODY TRACKDOWN #109	$2.75
__0-515-09445-5	LONGARM AND THE HANGMAN'S VENGEANCE #110	$2.75
__0-515-09491-9	LONGARM ON THE THUNDERBIRD RUN #111 (on sale March '88)	$2.75
__0-515-09520-6	LONGARM AND THE UTAH KILLERS #112 (on sale April '88)	$2.75

Please send the titles I've checked above. Mail orders to:

BERKLEY PUBLISHING GROUP
390 Murray Hill Pkwy., Dept. B
East Rutherford, NJ 07073

NAME_____
ADDRESS_____
CITY_____
STATE_____ZIP_____

Please allow 6 weeks for delivery.
Prices are subject to change without notice.
(Allow six weeks for delivery.)

POSTAGE & HANDLING:
$1.00 for one book, $.25 for each additional. Do not exceed $3.50.

BOOK TOTAL	$_____
SHIPPING & HANDLING	$_____
APPLICABLE SALES TAX (CA, NJ, NY, PA)	$_____
TOTAL AMOUNT DUE	$_____

PAYABLE IN US FUNDS.
(No cash orders accepted.)

☆ From the Creators of LONGARM ☆

The Wild West will never be the same!

LONE★STAR

LONE STAR features the extraordinary and beautiful Jessica Starbuck and her loyal half-American, half-Japanese martial arts sidekick, Ki.

___ LONE STAR ON THE TREACHERY TRAIL #1	08708-4/$2.50
___ LONE STAR AND THE LAND GRABBERS #6	08258-9/$2.50
___ LONE STAR IN THE TALL TIMBER #7	07542-6/$2.50
___ LONE STAR ON OUTLAW MOUNTAIN #11	08198-1/$2.50
___ LONE STAR AND THE GOLD RAIDERS #12	08162-0/$2.50
___ LONE STAR AND THE DENVER MADAM #13	08219-8/$2.50
___ LONE STAR AND THE MEXICAN STANDOFF #15	07887-5/$2.50
___ LONE STAR AND THE BADLANDS WAR #16	08199-X/$2.50
___ LONE STAR ON THE DEVIL'S TRAIL #20	07436-5/$2.50
___ LONE STAR AND THE MONTANA TROUBLES #24	07748-8/$2.50
___ LONE STAR AND THE AMARILLO RIFLES #29	08082-9/$2.50
___ LONE STAR ON THE TREASURE RIVER #31	08043-8/$2.50
___ LONE STAR AND THE MOON TRAIL FEUD #32	08174-4/$2.50
___ LONE STAR AND THE GOLDEN MESA #33	08191-4/$2.50
___ LONE STAR AND THE BUFFALO HUNTERS #35	08233-3/$2.50
___ LONE STAR AND THE BIGGEST GUN IN THE WEST #36	08332-1/$2.50

Available at your local bookstore or return this form to:

JOVE
THE BERKLEY PUBLISHING GROUP, Dept. B
390 Murray Hill Parkway, East Rutherford, NJ 07073

Please send me the titles checked above. I enclose _____. Include $1.00 for postage and handling if one book is ordered; add 25¢ per book for two or more not to exceed $1.75. CA, NJ, NY and PA residents please add sales tax. Prices subject to change without notice and may be higher in Canada. Do not send cash.

NAME_____
ADDRESS_____
CITY_____ STATE/ZIP_____

(Allow six weeks for delivery.)